P9-DZM-826

THE SECRET LIFE OF QUEEN VICTORIA.

THE SECRET LIFE OF QUEEN VICTORIA

HER MAJESTY'S MISSING DIARIES.

BEING AN ACCOUNT OF HER
HITHERTO UNKNOWN TRAVELS
THROUGH THE ISLAND OF JAMAICA
IN THE YEAR 1871.

EDITED AND LOYALLY ILLUSTRATED
BY

JONATHAN ROUTH

PUBLISHED BY
SIDGWICK AND JACKSON
LONDON.

Acknowledgements

The Editor would like to explain that some of the paintings he has used as illustrations in these pages are from the Collections of the persons of exquisite good taste who purchased them at past Exhibitions of his works. However, such is the Editor's lack of filing system, that he cannot work out who owns what picture. Therefore he trusts that the owners will pardon the liberty he has taken in reproducing them here without giving individual acknowledgements – and accept his thanks for their patronage.

First published in Great Britain in 1979
by Sidgwick & Jackson Limited

Designed by Paul Watkins

ISBN 0 283 98589 5 (Hard)
ISBN 0 283 98550 X (Limp)

Printed in Great Britain by
Loxley Brothers Limited
for Sidgwick & Jackson Limited
1 Tavistock Chambers, Bloomsbury Way,
London WC1A 2SG

Appleton
RUM
Victoria

Traditional Demonstration of Native Hospitality to Three New Arrivals.

Jonathan Routh '79

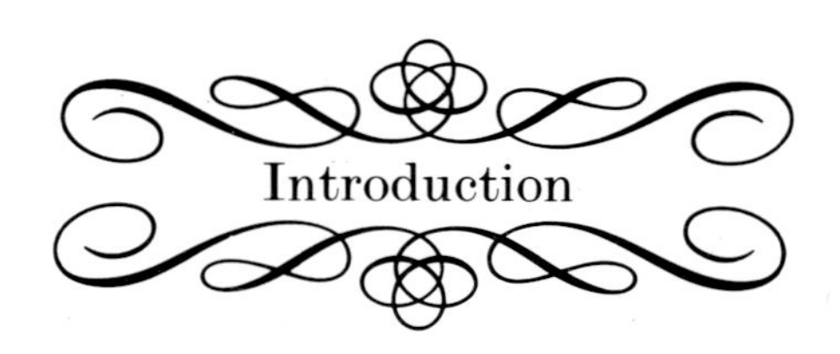

When I was a student of history at Emmanuel College, Cambridge, the generally-accepted theory regarding the three missing months in Queen Victoria's life (that is to say, the period between 22 March and 10 June 1871 that there is no *reliable* Journal of the Queen's to substantiate) was that she had retired to Osborne (later to Balmoral) in a sulk following one of her more serious altercations with her least favourite Prime Minister, Mr Gladstone. Certainly no two authoritative biographers of her reign have been able to produce quite the same story covering that period.

However, since 1971 we have had to reconsider the alternative that she retired to a very much farther part of the world than the Isle of Wight or Scotland.

Because in that year someone calling himself Lord Braborough saw fit to release to the *Observer* newspaper in London extracts from what he alleged was a Diary that Queen Victoria kept during her visit to Jamaica and which coincided with this empty period of her life.

The events described in this Diary seemed quite incredible – the Queen meeting up with a Circus, walking the tight-rope, being chased by lions, dining with a drunken Bishop under her table . . . When I was originally asked by the *Observer* to illustrate it (I think because I had some small reputation for painting Jamaica) I just couldn't believe that they could ever have been part of the life of our solid respectable Queen Victoria.

The way that the *Observer* and Lord Braborough explained it was thus:

At the beginning of 1871 the Queen, then aged fifty-one, was in a bad way. The life of a recluse she had led for the ten years since Prince Albert's death was under attack from all sides. To declare Blackfriars Bridge open had been her only public engagement in all 1870. The suggestion was made openly in print that in performing this simple ceremony she was hardly earning to the full the salary (£350,000 per annum) she was paid as Queen. In the streets factions agitated for abolition of the annual sums paid to her children and dependents. It was greatly to the Queen's annoyance, 'such *disloyal* sentiments'. At the same time Mr Gladstone was continually on at her about her going to live in Ireland for two months of each year as being her contribution to solving the Irish problem. She detested the thought of 'that man's machinations to make me live in a *bog*', and wrote back peremptorily to Gladstone, even hinting at abdication being 'the solution of *my* problem'.

On 21 March 1871, she again appeared in public, at Windsor, upon the marriage of her daughter Princess Louise to the Marquess of Lorne. And then she disappeared. That was the last occasion that her family, her Ministers or any of her people saw her for three months. During those three months bulletins were issued purporting to show she was confined with a nasal infection, first at Osborne, then when she was a little recovered and able to be moved, at Balmoral. There were people who swore they saw her at both Royal residences, and at the Albert Hall's opening on 29 March. But, the person they saw (according to Lord Braborough) was, in fact, Hamish or Patsy Brown (cousins of John's) or John Brown himself *made up to impersonate her*. The real Queen Victoria, using the *nom-de-plume* Mrs King, had sailed off to Jamaica immediately following her daughter's wedding, accompanied only by a Lt-Colonel Augustus Crosbie Maxwell and a Mrs Maud Beswick.

It was the most extreme, the most successful and most audacious effort to 'get away from it all' of the nineteenth century.

There had, of course, to be others in the plot. Near Royal Family had been informed and contrived to keep it secret. Sir William Jenner (the Queen's Personal Physician) had to know as the plotters relied on him to compose and issue bulletins about Her Majesty's health which could account for her absence from public appearances. But Mr Gladstone, to begin with, was *not* a party to it. When, through an indiscretion of a Member of the Prince of Wales's household at Sandringham, Gladstone discovered the subterfuge some two weeks after Victoria had been absent from the country, he realized he had no alternative but himself to become a party to the plot. He kept up the pretence of writing to his sovereign once a week at Osborne or Balmoral, but at the same time his first action was to detail a squadron of the West Indian Fleet under the command of Admiral Sir John Wyndham to proceed to Kingston immediately and 'to take all measures necessary to guard Her Majesty's Person and prevent the enemies of Her Majesty from seizing or in any way being propinquent to her *without Her Majesty knowing she is thus guarded*'.

That then is the background to the Diary that follows. How the Diary was discovered and why I believe it has to be authentic, and proof of one of the best-kept secrets of history, is a matter with which I will concern myself at its end.

J.R.

Mosquito Cove, April 1979

The Queen.

Bishop Kelso.

Colonel Maxwell.

Maud Beswick.

Out and About in the Streets of Kingston.

Our 3rd day in this strange land and I am constrained to risk the consequences & to take up my Journal again. As well, upon y'day's date Sir W. Jenner shd. have released his Bulletin* concerning the Growth in my Nose, thus accounting to my people for my seclusion & inconversability, at the same time providing a veil for my absence here.

We have been lodging since the packet docked† (and the Anguish & Sufferings of the voyage were brought to a merciful end) at Kingston, in a Women's Club‡ upon the waterfront, Maud (Beswick) as Miss Smith, Colonel Maxwell (housed in the Gentlemen's Annexe) as *Mister* Maxwell, and myself as I was on board the packet, as Mrs *King* – aliases which, so far, have left our true identities unexposed. I am sad to be without Brown, but his *Bashfulness* had exasperated me of late and he shd. be punished for it.

Insects (which have always been high upon my List of Detestations) abound, and of a most *impertinent* variety, causing havoc of my sleep with their noisy droning, and an unbecoming itchfulness (like an attack of the Fidgets) of my body. So while the heat – which I have never known the like of – has caused me to remove one of my undervests, I have donned gloves & veil to counter the attentions of the vindictive little bees.

---

*From the Court Circular of 10 April 1871 (but dated 9 April): 'Her Majesty the Queen is confined at Osborne House receiving treatment for a recurrence of the morbid grout-head in the left nostril which in the past has so adversely affected her breathing and speech. Her Majesty is most anxious that her Faithful Subjects should not Fret over her Condition which she can bear with fortitude knowing she is always in their prayers, and which the restful atmosphere and sea-air of her present accommodation alone can heal.'

†There is no mention in the Queen's Diary of her method of travelling to or from Jamaica. But it would seem likely from the examination of available passenger lists of sailing and steam vessels that, on the outward journey, her party was the 'Mrs King & Companions, 2' who boarded the Dutch steam vessel *Hendrijk van Haagen* at Plymouth on 24 March 1871. The vessel, bound from Amsterdam to Curaçao, would have taken fifteen days to reach Kingston in Jamaica – which fits the fact that the Queen's first diary entry is dated 10 April.

‡Jeffrey's Map of Kingston for 1880, which lists every building on the Kingston Waterfront, makes no mention of any 'Women's Club'. It was, then, one of the most notorious red-light areas of the whole Caribbean and it would seem most likely that, in her innocence of such matters, the Queen was inadvertently lodging at one of the establishments typical of the area. Possibly, going by Jeffrey's Map, Mrs Myrtle Bank's, or Peg's Club, or Madame Albertine's – none of them any longer in existence.

The Inconvenience of Lodging in the Vicinity of Persons of Low Origin.

The Right and Proper Way for a Person of Quality to Enter the Sea.

Our establishment noisy in the extreme in the evenings and have been constantly baffled at night by the gruffness of voice of some of the women Club members in the adjoining bedrooms – *so* gruff, had I not been told this was a *Women's* Club I would have thought they belonged to men (even men *of Low Origin*). Colonel Maxwell assured me I must be mistaken, that it was most likely hoarse-voiced Brothers & Cousins of the Ladies calling upon them & making sobbing farewells before departing for other lands. I suggested to the Col. that it must be very wearying to the Ladies to have so many Brothers & Cousins and asked him to find us alternate Lodgings where hoarse-voiced kinfolk might not be so numerous.

The Col. submitted that we should move to Mandeville where he enjoyed friends and where a gentler atmosphere reigned; and accordingly at eleven o'clock we set off for there in a hired carriage.

The journey long and not lacking in incident. Upon several occasions when sellers along the roadway would opportune us with their wares – fruits of such curious shapes and colours and bearing no recognisable relationship with our own dear English roots – Colonel Maxwell, over-fearful my person was being attacked, acted too hastily (I thought) with his guns. With each explosion Maud fainted and I had to wait impatiently several moments before directing her to throw some small purse to the survivors of the Colonel's unerring aim.

We passed through a countryside green – but not of the correct shade nor so well-ordered as Mine; and with a temperature I certainly should never have permitted. Indeed, fearful for the ill-effects of holding parasols over ourselves for such lengths of time, and so that we should not *all* be irreparably damaged from the exertion, I bade Maud to hold mine as well as her own over my body.

Many of the Estates we passed by, Colonel M informed me, (growing mostly bananas, and canes from which were fashioned sugar lumps – which struck me, even though I have never drunk a banana, as a most unnutritional combination such as only a very ignorant people could have devised) were owned by the scions of the great English families. I submitted to the Colonel that this was probably why they would always be scions, that the good God would not have put potatos and cabbages into the world unless He had intended us to live off Bubble and Squeak, and that anyone who had been given the privilege of cultivating His land and chose to ignore these noble fruits was doomed to remain as a scion or less.

The house we reached at Mandeville was that of the MacLissers,* old (but title-less) friends of Colonel Maxwell's (who had sent information ahead of our arrival). It was a pleasant if unsubstantial home – built of coloured woods and tin – with many balconies and pleasing prospects over the valley below, and the floor of every corridor lined with grovelling servants. We were shown to our rooms and allowed a sufficiency of time to rest and change before dinner was announced at 5 p.m. – Some 20 guests and tables laid with a display of foods such as I have not seen since leaving England – pies, pâtés, tarts, stews, legs of this and breasts of that – and every one of them Mr MacLisser proudly announced to us, of *goat* – which proclamation made me feel most faint and, famished though I was, I had to be seated at table pleading fullness and a need for a bowl of tea only – may God have understood and forgiven the untruth.

The MacLissers proved dull hosts. She with a vocabulary limited to the most banal commentary on the climatic conditions of the island during the last three hours – and in between, backing up both sides in any argument with polite grunts of agreement. (Also, poor woman, she had a long moustache and the deepest of voices.) And he, Mr MacLisser, infinitely more interested in the consumption of his claret than the demolition of his goat. He seemed engaged in competition of the liquid's consumption with the Reverend gentleman seated beside him (Bishop Kelso† from Kingston – who I certainly never remember having given such office to) so that before the end of the meal the both of them were spread upon the floor half concealed by the table-cloth and causing considerable hazard to the passing waiters. As I was a guest in this house, and more especially because I was in the guise of another person, I refrained from making my Face of Disapproval (but I shall certainly write a Strong Note to the Archbishop regarding Bishop Kelso's suitability for High Office).

---

* Evan MacLisser, a partner in the Warminster law-firm of Maxwell, Mobart and MacLisser, had won 2,000 acres of the Beckford Estate at Mandeville in a (very suspect) card-game with Thomas Beckford (whose Wiltshire estates the firm managed) in 1855. In Lady Abercrombie's *West Indian Days* (Doulton & Co. 1891) he is described as 'the most drunkennest man I ever met, whose custom it was each Christmas Eve to repair to a bath filled with over 20 gallons of Scotch Whiskey there to lie with his Estate Manager – a partly-coloured man – until the year's end, his wife withdrawing to Kingston or sometimes Havana to leave the two of them alone in the consumption of the bath's alcoholic content, and instructing the family doctor to look at their condition each 72 hours'.

Dainties, the MacLisser house, was demolished in 1962 when the extension to the airstrip at Mandeville was constructed – but the stones alongside the northern perimeter of the new runway are from the old Beckford rum distillery.

It is difficult to understand why Colonel Maxwell thought Evan MacLisser would be a suitable host for the Queen, excepting on the grounds of his own kinship with MacLisser's partner in Warminster.

†The name of 'Bishop' Kelso occurs in many West Indian Memoirs between 1860 and 1890. But he was far from being anyone that at any time the Queen had appointed as one of her Bishops. His real name was James Alexander Kilpin, the only British Army officer to have deserted while on active service during the Crimean War. He made his way then, disguised as an Armenian monk, from Sebastopol to Copenhagen whence he shipped to the (then) Danish-owned West Indian Island of St Croix. On the neighbouring island of Grenada he founded the Church of the Blessed Kelso which he administered from sumptuous premises on Mount Royal in St George's. By the time of Queen Victoria's arrival in the Caribbean he had been in Jamaica for over six years, enjoying the full confidence of Government and planters alike. His subsequent history is clouded with his alcoholism and he died in conditions of some penury in Palm Beach, Florida, in 1895.

A Performance by Blind Bell-Ringers outside Mr Wade's Rented House at Ocho Rios.

There was however one guest I found of most pleasing behaviour, and had he not claimed to be an American I would most certainly have thought him to be a Gentleman. This was a Mr Arnold Wade who was seated upon the other side of me to Colonel Maxwell and who informed me he was the proprietor of a Circus which he had brought to Jamaica to train and re-organise before opening with it in his native Boston in the late Summer.

It was more difficult when Mr Wade – in the forthright manner that I have discovered Americans favour – made polite enquiries concerning my own person and background. I spoke generally – of being a widow living in the Home Counties of England (but with an address in London); and the late Mr King I answered to a further enquiry, had worked for the government in an administrative capacity.

The goat feast thankfully came to its end and after Colonel Maxwell had suggested to our host he persuade Maud to sing in the withdrawing room we were able to make our excuses and retire to our rooms.

The night not lightly spent by me, for the odour of goat pervaded every corner of the house, the barking of dogs outside quite drowned the accustomed silence of darkness, and as no-one came to stop it Maud continued her screaming until the early hours.

In my wakefulness I thought much of Mr Wade, for in his thoughtfulness and commanding manner I saw reflected certain of the qualities of my beloved Albert.

Arnold Wade

Tuesday April 11th

Maud brought me my Tea & Biscuit at 6 a.m. and on the tray a letter that emanated from the pen of Mr Wade and which invited us to stay with him – for as long as we should wish – at his rented home in Ocho Rios. – It is still an excitement for me to realise that, being in the guise of Mrs King, and without Appointment & Protocol, I am at liberty to accept such invitations without delay.

I replied happily, saying we would arrive in whatever length of time it took to travel from Mandeville to this place.

At 7 a.m. at first breakfast downstairs (goat chops, goat kidneys on toast, jerk goat with ackee whatever that may have been I took just another bowl of tea) I learnt that Mr Wade had already departed to put his house in order for our arrival. I appraised Colonel Maxwell of the arrangements I had made and thought he seemed a trifle disapproving of the idea – no doubt because the previous night there had been talk of some hunting – the Colonel's favourite sport – over our host's property this day.

By 8 a.m. our carriage was on its way again. By Skull Point, Bethany, Balaclava, Auchtembeddie, Wait-A-Bit, Joe Hut, Barbecue Bottom and Runaway we drove before reaching Ocho Rios on the coast at dusk. Colonel Maxwell had occasion to assassinate only one person along the route – a poor old fellow full of drink who brandished a long knife at us after our carriage accidentally overturned his four female companions, and for whom the Colonel's shot must have proved a Merciful Release.

Mr Wade, more handsome than I recollected him upon the yesterday, stood welcoming upon his house's porch, himself conducted us to our rooms, bade us descend if and as when we so wished to a dinner downstairs. Too tired for food, I regretfully declined, but Maud went down and this time my night was made hideous not just by her screamings but also by the roars and cries of wild animals that seemed all around us.

– I should have been opening a waterworks in Aberdeen this day. I shall make it up to the Mayor with a portrait of Me in a *real* silver frame.

A Prudent Approach to a New Acquaintance.

In the Company of Interesting New Friends.

With daylight I was able to see the beauty of our situation – reminding me much of the I. of Wight – a well-appointed wood house at the mouth of a fast flowing river and an endless number of stablings and outhouses along its banks – from these it must have been did emanate the jungle sounds that had so disturbed my night. Though still with fatigue following yesterday's long & hot journey, and would have preferred to lie reading the papers lazily all morning, I accepted Mr Wade's invitation after 1st Breakfast to show us round his property, to wonder at his elephants, lions, zebras and the like. He introduced us, too, to the performers of his Circus (some of whom I must admit only slightly approximated to the human shape) Miss Biggy the Fat Lady, Wing and Wong the Two Midgets, and others who practised their craft upon high wires strung between the trees. When one would fall Mr Wade would admonish the fellow for his carelessness and advise him his pay was docked until such time as he could walk again.

– Again, Mr Wade's commanding manner put me in mind of my beloved Albert. One thing only on this day marred my increasing happiness which was that we lost Maud during the morning. She had wished to see the lions again but in some manner her presence so excited the beasts – she was singing heavily at the time – they broke from their cages and accosted our party. Then after observing the beasts consume Maud so completely I felt it a prudent precaution, concerning my own person, to take cover in a juniper tree. And thus I waited – in prayer – until Colonel M, limping bravely from the wounds he had suffered, was able to shoo the lions back to their cage; and Mr Wade, hobbling also and dishevelled like a common Fifeshire scarecrow, came – profuse with apologies over the consumption of Maud; but I as profuse to him over the provocation she had given his beasts. Poor Maud, she will be missed in Norfolk. She had on her at the time the stockings I gave her last Lady Day.

The rest of the day quite without excitement. Mr Wade presented me with a leopard cub that I shall call Towser, and a coloured maidservant already called Miss Pearly, who will bring me morning tea and dress me. Bishop Kelso turned up at dinner – he had been lingering under the table since luncheon it appeared, and Mr Wade, having complimented me on my agility in ascending juniper trees asked if I should like to experience one of his tight-ropes on the morrow. I replied that I thought not.

Thursday April 13th

Mr Wade offered us at 1st Breakfast the alarming information that in the eve Sir John Peter Grant the Governor would be dining with us after opening the new Free School at St Anne's. He surely (for he lunched at Windsor 11 yrs ago after I had knighted him for his career in the Indian Service) must be the last person I should encounter! Already it is become hampering in the street of Ocho Rios – those persons who stop and stare after me as though they *know* me but cannot quite place *where* they met me – even one good lady who, while holding in one hand an envelope with a postage stamp from England upon it, accosted me in the haberdashers to say, but was she not mistaken that I was the model for some portrait she had seen but recently but the title to which she had since forgot. I replied, as deeply as my voice would let me, 'Alas *but* No, Madame – *but* Captain Addams of the Kingston Light Infantry disguised because on active service *but* always at *your* service!' – The poor thing went straight into a faint and had to be revived with the haberdasher's salts. So after breakfast I enquired of Col. Maxwell if he did not think it prudent that I should withdraw with the works of Sir W. Scott to the shelter of my room all this day – or with the excuse of finger-ache – to avoid the danger of further recognition, and most particularly the gaze of Sir J. Grant. Col. M. admitted that, had I asked him but 10 minutes previous, he would have complimented me on my plan, but that in that intervening time I had already been espied by Sir J. – come early to keep his appointment and who had witnessed my exit from breakfast on to the verandah to drain my bowl of stinking goat-slops – so not to hurt Mr Wade's sensitive feelings – into his poinsettia pots. And Sir J., in a state of amazement & confusion, had approached him (Col. M.) for corroboration of what his eyes caused him to suspect, and he (Col. M.) had felt himself helpless but to admit the truth – being unwilling to deceive one who once had been a brother officer. This being so I realised I could hardly blame Colonel Maxwell, and told him to produce, and bind to secrecy, Sir J. without delay. Briefly, I explained to Sir J. the circumstances of my situation and as quickly, being no sympathiser of Mr Gladstone's either, he offered me the use of Queen's House in Kingston and what else I needed. He was, I suspect, taken aback when I answered that my needs were simple, a Chaplain upon Sundays, and the use of any Band he might control upon occasional afternoons (for I have long wished to conduct such a Body of Men). Sir J. assured me a Band would be at my beck from to-morrow after-

Taking Steps to Avoid a Nasty End.

The Usefulness of Umbrellas While Travelling Across Country.

noon on, and also a certain Bishop Kelso who could be my Sunday Chaplain. I replied I had already met this certain Bishop Kelso and had formed doubts about the man's suitability for any profession other than that of a wine-bibber but that if Sir J. recommended him then I should be happy to reconsider my doubts.

Our meeting ended with Sir John promising to produce the Bishop at dinner that night, and my extracting from Sir John the promise he would tell no person, and especially not Mr Wade or any member of Mr Wade's household, my true identity.

Passed the remainder of the day, as I had intended, with Sir W. Scott in my room and on my verandah until dinner when much amused by Sir John's embarrassment while Mr Wade addresses me as 'Mrs King Old Fruit'. – Poor Sir John, powerless through his promise to me, to take action against what he must consider as the Humiliation of his Sovereign. I shall find if there is a Garter available for him upon my return.

A wet, misty, most *threatening* morning! It was the same (though not so humid with it) once or twice in former happy days, and my dear Albert, if I complained, always said we could not alter it, but must leave it as it was, and make the best of it. How wise he was, and how amiss am I in failing to have presented to a wider public (which could surely benefit from it) a collection of his *wisdom*. Wanting to exorcise my mood I wrote a rude note to Mr Gladstone about his Match Tax and afterwards felt much, *much* improved.

Kelso at dinner sank below the table-cloth with his accustomed third bottle of claret and stayed there the evening terrorising the table-servants, snapping at their ankles as they passed and growling angrily over their bodies when they fell. Despite the combined remonstrations of Colonel Maxwell and Mr Wade, the Bishop would not be deterred from this occupation; and it, becoming increasingly violent and noisy as one table-servant after another was accumulated in a pitiful cowering heap beside the serving-board, the rest of us withdrew to consume our trifles in peace upon the verandah.

A letter from dear Alix via Sir John this a.m. The children are well and Bertie is ensconced at Sandringham supervising the building operations. The Wretch Gladstone is still obviously considering that I should spend part of my year in Ireland as he has asked the D. of Leinster whether he would be willing to surrender his seat. Wrote back a p.c. to Alix repeating I will NOT end my days in an Irish *bog*, and asking if (concerning Sandringham) Bertie was convinced 180 bedrooms would be enough.

Following Bishop Kelso's curiously canine behaviour last night at dinner we are without table-servants in the household until Mr Wade and the Col. return from the hills with whatever number they can catch there. For my contribution to our communal well-being, poached my own egg for luncheon, then took soap to the river to clean my stays & stomachers & the gentlemen's unmentionables. Then, returning to the house, found a group of splendidly-uniformed blackies with musical instruments waiting there – their leader with instructions from Sir J. Grant that I should consider them available to lead withersoever I wished. Led them backwards and forwards through the house then through the house of Ld. Pringle across the river who, poor man, had a fit at seeing us pass through his bedroom and down his stairs. Then led my Band for a further 3 hours o'er hill and dale:

Nature's music from the birds and flowers
Could not compete with tunes like ours

– dear Sir W. Scott, he would have appreciated the spectacle most gladly. Afterward requested and was given a further hour's instruction in the art of tuba-playing. Felt much *puffed* at the end.

Bishop Kelso at dinner on about *Hunting*. It is, he declares, a most excellent *Sabbath* occupation. But when I asked for *before* Matins or for *after* Matins he replied for *during* Matins and that it used to be his custom when he had the living of Mandeville to place upon the Church door a sign saying Closed on Sundays and take to the field with as many of his parishioners as

Helping Out During a Domestic Crisis.

The Pleasures of a Stroll with Musical Accompaniment.

could assemble a horse together. Then when I expressed my surprise that foxes should live on the island he replied Oh, no, it was not foxes he hunted, but blackies. – I chided him for making sport of such a quarry and told him that next time – for Mr Arnold Wade appeared at this moment – he should take his pick of one of Mr Wade's beasts and pursue *it*. Mr Wade, kind and generous man that he is, immediately volunteered to donate the Bishop with a leprous cheetah for his sport, and it was arranged that on the morrow the Boscobel Riders would pursue the unfortunate beast. Agreed to accompany the riders and passed the remainder of the morning, until my Band came for me to lead, with Col. Maxwell and Mr Wade in the inspection of suitable mounts. Led the band half as far as Boscobel then grew weary of the diversion – for to-day I played the drum around my middle – and instructed them to seek out a House of Refreshment while I repaired home.

Monday April 17th

All assembled at 8 in the morning outside the Boscobel Weigh House for the Hunt to move off. – The most motley assembly of mounts. My good self side-saddled on the large horse called Wilberforce that Col. M. and I had chosen out of Mr Wade's stables on the yesterday, Col. M. below me on Tipsy Maisie, the little Shetland whose prowess on the Hunting field I was curious to discover: while Mr Wade himself trailed 2 Zebras to induct them into the sport. – And even more motley was the collection of dogs passing as Hounds – more like 50 Mongrels taken at random from a Home.

Bishop Kelso I noted most unsteady in his saddle – indeed, he was removed from it within a mile of our moving off and after Mr Wade had instructed his leprous cheetah to be loosed. The country we rode over in pursuit of the beast not unlike Aberdeenshire, but with more palm trees. The mongrels all disappeared immediately & in all directions, and poor Colonel M. struck his head against a coconut – more correctly, he was felled by a falling nut and for want of a stretcher needed dragging back to the house still not having regained his consciousness. The leprous beast run to earth at half past one o'clock by a banana wharf on the beach by Oracabessa, where Mr Wade gave orders for a group of blackies armed with machetes to despatch it; and there the beast after first demolishing some 5 of the blackies, more indolent and less agile than their fellows, met its just end.

– Much exhausted pleasurably by the day's exercise, and with much admiration for Mr Wade's seat as a rider & his resolution as a *man*. No obstacle too daunting for him to essay – fences, gates & walls he drove over with a consummate ease. At one point when a blackie remonstrated that the Hunt had driven through and laid flat his crop of yams & caused to fall down the pitiful collection of old boards and posts he referred to as his *home* Mr Wade descended from his saddle and, for this *impertinence*, gave the fellow a thorough thrashing with his bare hands – then, for compensation of his yams & home, pressed a florin piece into the unconscious man's hand.

– Am continually encouraged by being in the presence of such a *man* – & whose many little courtesies still fill me with gt. pleasure. Even this eve at dinner, when the golden syrup was spilt over my head-dress Mr Wade was the first at table to drench his napkin in his Chablis wine and take action to remove the offending sweet-stuff.

Col. M. still unconscious by my bed-time so requested Mr Wade to summon a Doctor upon the morrow.

The doctor when he arrived to inspect Col. Maxwell opined that the Col. had received a blow to the head that had rendered him unconscious and that there was nothing to be done for him until consciousness returned which could be in any length of time at all. After his visit was walking out (determined to implement my colouring by use of the sun so wearing very little) with only Towser as company when time and time again I overheard rustlings from the bushes as though some creatures of Mr W's were there *lurking*. Once I turned my head from whence came these noises and thought I saw some black-headed *Thing*. So to distract my mind from what it could have been I started thinking Great and Beautiful Thoughts – like what would happen if everybody in England, Wales and Scotland were to sing God Save the Queen at exactly midday every Sunday; or what would happen if Mr Gladstone lost his voice and was confined to his room with a mysterious ailment of the knees for the rest of his life; and how many presents I would have if everyone in England, Wales and Scotland had to give me one on my Birthday.

Towser and I turned about only half the distance we had intended to penetrate into the jungle and, returning to the house, I dressed & reported

The Healthful Activity of Walking One's Cheetah.

In Pursuit of a Leprous Cheetah.

my unease to Mr W. who swore he was missing no Black-headed Thing from his menagerie, and nor, he also swore, were any Black-headed Things indigenous to this part of Jamaica save the Black Bowler, a nearly-black butterfly with a span of a mere three inches.* He suggested that to further distract myself from the experience I go out on the sands beside the house and use his pedal-pram – a curious little device like an enclosed bicycle, motivated by pressing with one's feet on little pedals. One of the rhinos ran amok during this exercise & charged at me, but I was too wily for him with my steering of the machine and, after an hour of charging, the beast grew tired and retired silently to its cage. Will mention the device to the D. of Cambridge for possible issue to one of the new cavalry regiments.

In the eve information that the Band I had abandoned on the road to Boscobel still waited at the House of Refreshment for my instruction, though they are all weak, some in fact barely conscious through consuming overdoses of some beverage served on the premises without taking the precaution of accompanying it with sufficient foodstuff. 2 Tuba-players had even run amok and for a whole morn played their instruments, much to the detriment of Justice, on the roof of the Court-House at Port Maria.

I sent a note bidding them retrieve their tuba-players and all return to Sir J. Grant in Kingston.

Mr Wade said at dinner (goat curry but no Bishop Kelso) that a propos this temporary disability of the Col's if there was any service he could perform for my good self like *Lifting* Heavy Objects (such as on several occasions the Col. had done for me when such objects had got in my way), or *guarding* my Valuables, or *taking charge* of my Exchequer, that I should not hesitate to call upon him. I thanked him gratefully, and afterwards retired to ponder more on this kind man's thoughtfulness.

Wednesday April 19th

Colonel M. is still not come to, so turned to Mr. W. to discuss with him a matter that otherwise I wd. have brought up with the Col – to wit, *my size*. – For I have been expanding at such a rate on the diet of goat curry & rice

*The rustlings that the Queen heard on this walk were without doubt caused by the lurking of sailors of the West Indian Fleet following Mr Gladstone's orders to 'guard her Majesty's Person . . . without Her Majesty knowing she is thus guarded'. At the short notice they were given to go into action it is unlikely that they could have obtained any disguises more elaborate than the normal clothing sold in the stores and tailors shops of Kingston – the tail-coats with bowlers or top-hats which Jamaicans were so addicted to wearing at this time. Still, the thought of 200 men so garbed, lurking in the undergrowth, – possibly blacked-up as well – is a sobering one. And there is reason to believe that on subsequent occasions many of them were dressed in bonnets and crinolines.

that is served to us 4 times a day in this household that I felt I should make an earnest effort to Dwindle & Taper at certain points. Mr Wade opined that exercising upon the machines at the military encampment at Boscobel could be my remedy. So, to that we repaired. – The Swing not remedial enough I thought. – Nor the running jumping and somersaulting machine really suited to maintain the dignity of one of my years. – But then a most marvellous and novel machine. One climbed to its top by means of a foot-ladder, and then slid down it on one's back. It is a most wondrous sensation, and a most fine feat of engineering that it could almost, I thought, have been devised by Mr Brunel. (I have made a sketch of it to show him upon my return.) – Then to the one-wheeler which I found I could be master of for but seconds at a time. – And finally, at the suggestion of some watching bandsmen, to the *hoop* – not wheeling it along in the conventional manner, but attempting to keep it in movement around one's body. (Alas! attempting to keep time to the bandsmen playing Mr Mendelssohn's new Symphony was a very great strain upon *my* poor wracked body!!!)

Afterwards, still of the opinion that this exercising had not caused me to Dwindle enough, I enjoined Mr Wade to organise a ball game with the bandsmen. We played by *my* Rules and I was very victorious – my joy only being diminished when Randy the Cook arrived with the news that Towser has been consumed by a passing crocodile. I asked Mr Wade to have his remains packed and placed by my bedside (for some day I shall transfer them to my Pets Last Resting-Place in Hyde Park).

A most curious incident this morning. Was engaged in practising my toe dancing in the new shoes that Mr Wade had had the smith in town construct for me when a long procession, all of it wailing and chanting, arrived before the house bearing a coffin which they placed upon the doorstep and then settled down beside wailing and chanting all the louder. It being a fair inconvenience to enter and exit from the house while climbing over this encumbrance I was curious as to its purpose and from Miss Pearly I elicited the most bizarre explanation. The body in the coffin was that of the late Mr Joel of Ocho Rios, a supplier of animal feeds; and when the mourners came to take him to his place of burial they had heard coming from the coffin the words of Mr Joel that he was owed money by Mr Wade

An Unexpected Meeting on the Sands.

Learning to Lose Weight with Dignity.

and would be unable to rest in peace until such sum was paid to his survivors. This, Miss Pearly assured me, was the custom of the country – that if any corpse imparted such information it should rest on the doorstep of his debtor until the sum was paid.

At that moment Mr Wade advanced apologetically into the withdrawing room where I was seated with Miss Pearly and asked for a word in confidence with me. Dismissing Miss Pearly I listened as Mr Wade confirmed her tale and asked would it be possible that I could be of temporary assistance to him as the postal services had failed to deliver to him a draft from Boston he had been expecting and he did not have enough money upon his person to pay off the companions of the corpse upon his doorstep. It would, he assured me, be only a matter of days before he was able to refund me. Oh poor Mr Wade that he should have to need to be bothered with such trivia when his great mind was engaged in so many worthy projects! I assented immediately to his request, assuring him it was my privilege to be of help to him and repaired to my room to draw the notes* which would enable free entrance and egress through the front door.

Later in the day while perambulating through the town I glimpsed the same mourners and survivors of the animal-feed supplier dancing grotesquely and noisily, Mr Wade in their midst, outside a beach-side tavern. – It is indeed an island of the *strangest* customs.

Colonel M. still in exactly the same position as when I last visited him. The poor Col. – he had worked hard for me and must need the rest.

Concerning the exercise Mr Wade had planned for the benefit of my Dwindling & Tapering to-day I passed the morning receiving instruction in the art of tightrope-walking from some of Mr Wade's clowns, and this afternoon out in the jaunting cart to Mr Dunn's Falls nearby to attempt the public rope. Bishop Kelso, swaying only ever so slightly, said a very beautiful prayer before my attempt, and all seemed much relieved at its successful conclusion. I must remember to tell Mr Brunel that walking on

*The accounts of the Royal Family are private so there is no real way of knowing how much the Queen – or, more likely, Colonel Maxwell on her behalf – was carrying. Also, there were no Exchange Regulations in those days to record or restrict the amount (and no Passports). But from the sums the Queen states in her Diary that she handed at various times to Arnold Wade she must have had with her a minimum of £20,000 – worth about £$\frac{1}{2}$m. in today's money.

At the other end of the scale, her berth from Plymouth to Kingston is unlikely to have cost her more than £11.

a tightrope is a very good way of crossing a waterfall without getting wet (but that walking down a ladder forwards is not a very good way of walking down a ladder; perhaps he could design one that you walk down *backwards*).

After dinner my great pleasure to accede to Mr W's request that I might advance him a further £500 for food for his kangaroos as his moneys were still not arrived from Boston.

But later, while writing my Journal, it occurred to me I had not noted any kangaroos in Mr W's menageries. Determined to tax him upon the subject on the morrow.

When, at 1st Breakfast, I enquired of Mr Wade concerning his kangaroos he said that alas, a great tragedy had occurred during the night. All the food he had fed them – rushed to the house by the survivors of the late animal-food man of Ocho Rios – had been poisoned and all the kangaroos had died. He was just back from burning them and now, he explained, he was in need of a further £500 to repair the Pagoda in the Gardens which the kangaroos, in their death-throes, had kicked down. Seeing little reason why this kind man's mind should be plagued by such trivia I once again advanced him the sum he required and immediately received from him an invitation to inspect his latest piece of equipment just arrived on the boat from New Orleans, a cannon that ejects human beings into the atmosphere. He had assembled it on the other side of the river to the rented house, and to there we repaired after breakfast. A most splendidly unwarlike instrument of war it turned out to be, decorated all over with a motif of rosebuds and violets. What pleasure it could be to campaign with such an instrument! (Memo to the Wretch Gladstone upon return – or better, to the D. of Cambridge, – suggesting allowance be made in the forthcoming Army Estimate for decoration of our own dear British guns like this. Suggest it would be an actual *economy* as my enemies would be quite *stunned* at the beauty of such artillery and our battles could be won without firing any single shot.)

– Complimented Mr Wade on his taste in such a purchase but when I requested him for a demonstration of it he was reluctant – explaining it had arrived without full instructions for firing it. Explained to him (which fortunately he did not query, nor ask in what circumstances) that I had

A Novel Way of Crossing a Waterfall Without Getting Wet.

A Novel Way of Entering the Sea.

been witness to many thousands of cannon being fired in my time, and that if his men will follow *my* instructions and fill the base of the machine with gunpowder (or its local equivalent) *I* would then demonstrate the cannon's capabilities. Miss Pearly made strong remonstrance that I should not involve myself in the experiment but I insisted, placing myself in the cannon's barrel, and instructing Mr Wade how to ignite the powder.

– It was a most *odd* sensation being ejected through the air, describing what I believe men of mathematics would call a *parabola* through it, and viewing what was below as from a bird's eye. How long I was in the air I could not estimate – later some said half a minute and some a minute and a half. My landing (to which I had given no previous thought) was in the sea, and some of Mr Wade's clowns who were gambolling on a beach nearby, amid much laughing and *guffawing*, waded in to pull me shorewards. A most *salutary* experience, and afterwards Mr Wade kind enough to offer me regular employment with his Circus repeating my feat *twice daily*.

Then at dinner Mr Wade repeated this kind offer, emphasising that he made it in all seriousness, drawing a fine picture of life as a performer in a Circus, and adding that if I should wish to invest a sum of £5000 with him he could see to it that my name as a performer could become known all over the Americas. I thanked him again and handed him this sum saying only that I should like it to be a contribution toward what I expected the cost of his Cannon to be.

But once again, when later on I was completing my Journal, I pondered upon the other matter that Mr Wade had introduced into our conversation earlier in the day, the Pagoda that he claimed his kangaroos had destroyed. For assuredly in my wanderings of the Gardens I had seen no such building. However, I am really become quite enamoured of this way of life, so different to my old. I think it will teach the Wretch Gladstone the biggest lesson of his miserable life if I accede to Mr Wade's remarkable offer.

I was become quite concerned over Colonel Maxwell's failure to move for such a length of time now and asked Mr Wade if he felt we should see a 2nd Opinion upon his state. But Mr Wade opined that we should not interfere with the Course of Nature and that unless we heard the Col. crying in pain we should leave him to his rest and not worry ourselves unduly. He also repeated to me his offer of some time earlier that if, during the Col's immobility, I should feel need of some other person to look after my Exchequer then I should feel most free to call upon his services. I thanked Mr Wade and said that I did not wish to trouble him with further responsibilities than he already had with his Circus.

And then I asked Mr Wade if, as a reward for my services to his cannon, he would let me don the eagles' wings he had in his Collection. He replied he would prefer not to take the responsibility with my body but would try to persuade one of his grooms to demonstrate them. Some 2 hours of persuasion later, the man, having donned them, then climbed to the summit of the small promontory beside us, launched himself off it – and *plummeted* like a stone straight down at our feet. I pointed out that the poor broken wretch's failure was because he had not studied *flapping* sufficiently, and, the wings being disengaged from his body, I requested they should be strapped to mine. Observed by a group of grey-clad men who had just previously appeared on the scene – an outing of undertakers from Kingston, Mr Wade informed me – I then launched myself off the top of this same promontory, flapping in a *proper* manner – it being my intention to execute two circles around the heads of the undertakers and land on my feet in front of Mr Wade. *But* just then a disloyal gust of wind sprang up, and even as I launched myself it caused me too to plummet. Thinking this to be my end – a bold one for Mrs King, if one without precedent for any Queen of England – I immediately went into prayer but opening my eyes some moments later found to my relief I had landed softly – as I had intended – right in front of Mr Wade – though if not upon my feet but the base of my back AND *in a net* – held all round by grinning undertakers. I did not understand, I complained to Mr Wade – but he was evasive. Why, I asked, should undertakers be bearing such a net? And why should undertakers bearing such a net be passing by that very moment? It was their fishing tackle they were just preparing to cast, said Mr Wade. But his tone did not convince me.

And now I pen my Journal I still wonder on the coincidence of that moment. I am wondering too whether so many aerial journeys as I seem to be making upon this island (and there is still Mr Wade's balloon to use) will entitle me to add to the titles I already bear that of *'Queen of the Fairies'* – though perhaps dear Bertie would not be so happy to inherit such.

A Helpful Form of Transport When One is Tired of Walking.

An Exhibition of Plummeting (Attended by a Group of Undertakers).

Monday April 24th

Such a great surprise this morning! Sir Edwin Landseer arrived – come, he explained, in dear Alix's confidence to execute my portrait for Bertie's coming birthday. How thoughtful of dear Alix, and what a wise and *sensible* choice of present! Sir E., looking very old and grey – almost *at bay* – & saying time was not his servant, produced his crayons and travelling rocking-stag forthwith. I told him that, as it were for Bertie, this should not be a conventional portrait, and that it would surely amuse Bertie to see his mother wearing a *wanton* air. Sir E. replied he had little experience in the portrayal of libertines, but would endeavour to execute my wish. I adopted a pose which I thought would provide the necessary inspiration, but – alas! – the sketch Sir E. showed me after two hours was one of such sanctimonious dullness it could have been overlooked in any *church*. Sir Edwin, I had to decide, though my dearest Albert so greatly admired his work, is nothing but an old *faddy-daddy*. When he had left, I set to work myself to make the sort of portrait I would have had him execute. I signed it 'V. King' and made a note to instruct Col. M, when he was revived, to place it in the next year's Academy.

Mr Wade made the request at dinner that I should advance him a further £1000 for dentistry to his rhinoceros. When I complained that this seemed an unreasonably large sum to pay to a mere tooth-puller Mr Wade said it was not going to the tooth-puller but to the man's widow, and, comprehending, I asked no more and advanced Mr W. the sum.

Tuesday April 25th

Was swinging through the forest – which I had chosen as to-day's exercise for my Dwindling – when Bishop Kelso processed by. The temptation was too great! 'Me Mrs King!' I proclaimed as I alighted out of the trees on top of him. His processors (young bottle-carriers I suspected) fled, and I after them. Then, at dinner, I denied the whole affair. When the Bishop injected the subject into conversation, I suggested to the company the poor man was having delusions – for I had passed the whole day sketching by the riverside (I said). The Bishop left half his 3rd bottle of claret unfinished and retired to the rooms prepared for him forthwith. (I suspect my fibbing may yet cure his addiction!)

Wednesday April 26th

General Plummett of the United States Army is a guest at dinner to-night for, Mr Wade tells us, he and I will travel to Port Antonio on the morrow with the General as our pilot *by balloon*. – Much excited by the prospect, for the idea of moving from one point to another over the earth's surface *in a laundry basket* is as near an invention of genius as the world has yet known. Read well into the night, and pondered upon the sanity of Sir Walter Scott.

Thursday April 27th

Such disappointment! The trip by balloon to Port Antonio cancelled on account General Plummett has decided it would be imprudent for our safety to place our trust in to-day's high winds. I tell Mr Wade that, having become so excited by the prospect, I would rather wait until the winds are righted than travel there by boat or carriage.

Spent the day writing more post-cards to the children – a large one to Freddie of Hesse whose birthday looms – another to Brown reminding him to repair the jogging cart.

Much amused to read in the newspaper (*The Gleaner* and De Cordova's *Advertising Sheet*) an announcement concerning *Osborne* & Co's Real Old Brown *Windsor* Soap!!! A packet would surely make an admirable gift to take back to the staff. The paper also announces that Paris is divested and Notre Dame sacked. Poor Louis – I do wish Vicky would restrain Fritz from his pugnacious ways.

Friday April 28th

At last! General Plummett has proclaimed the winds are suitable to our departure by balloon for Port Antonio. After prayers for our safety had been mumbled by Bishop Kelso, and after Miss Pearly's *umpteenth* entreaty that I should not submit myself to this uneasy form of transportation, Mr Wade, the General and myself took to our basket and ascended from the nearby sands. A most *alarming* sensation to begin with, but the

Adopting a Pose for Sir E.

Painting Oneself as One Prefers to See Oneself.

beauty of the prospects we looked down upon & the extraordinary *silence* of the atmosphere made it an experience unforgettably worthwhile. Much intrigued by the General's system of steering us which he claimed to be doing by ejecting overboard particles of sand from a bag with a small silver spoon – how splendidly is Science progressed in my time and how right was Albert to have so encouraged it.

Our descent at Port Antonio unremarkable. Met by many dignitaries and passed the night at the house of one of them, Mr Remarkable Flynn.

Saturday April 29th

Port Antonio is a most beautifully sited place (when the rains abate and permit one to see it), and peculiar in that all inhabitants bear the one name, the same as our host's, that of *Flynn*. We are come here, Mr Wade now informs us, for himself to find a rare hedge-pig in the hills nearby which he can display in his Circus; and for me (in my capacity as a visiting Englishwoman of good connection – and nobody knowing my true identity) to unveil an Obelisk – erected by Public Subscription – to my dearest Albert. Mr Remarkable Flynn, with great courtesy, escorted me to the ceremony at Flynn's Pleasure Gardens, & I performed the duty with very real pleasure, the statuary being quite worthy of my Angel. – Oh, how I wished I could reveal myself and so impress the company by my kinship with this noble man!

The aftermath of the ceremony, with much refreshment and conversing, too much of an emotional ordeal for me and I needed to be escorted away by Mr Wade to privacy. The evening read, and pondered upon the sanity of Lord Tennyson.

Sunday April 30th

Again by balloon – but not so successfully as before. We – just the General and myself – ascended from a promontory off the town but so immersed had we both become in the picture-books Mr Wade had provided for our diversion in the sky that 20 minutes later we did not note a loss of height our laundry basket was suffering and suddenly were buffeted into the side of a gorge. There being 30 or so feet of tree between ourselves and the ground at our final resting-place we had to wait for Mr Wade's arrival with laddering before disembarking in any dignified manner. We *rafted* our way back to the river's mouth and from thence took carriage back to town. Decided *not* to look at picture-books when making balloon ascents in future.

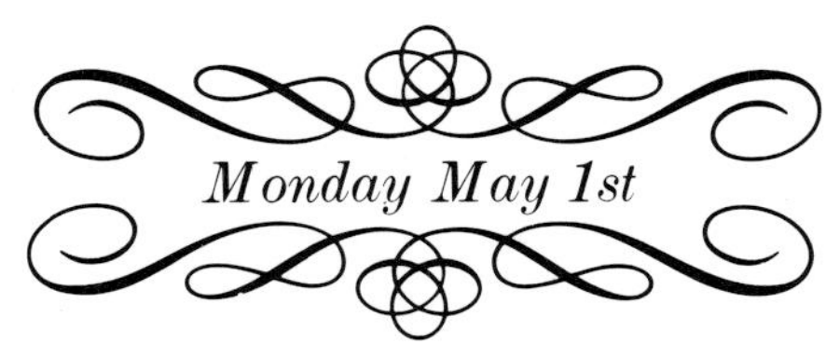

To-day Mr Wade had promised me experience in a novel form of aquatic progress peculiar to these parts. We rode by zebra to Blue Hole, a mystic lake connected to the sea, and there Mr Wade fastened to my feet curved beams of wood, instructed me to hold with my hands a rope attached to the helm of a paddle boat, and then *launched* me into the water. Alas! I overturned immediately – and several times more before staying successfully upright and speeding through the seas upon my feet.

Afterwards – mindful that previously only Our Lord had thus progressed upon the waters with any degree of success – I enquired of Bishop Kelso if such imitative action might not be a blasphemy. The Bishop thought not if I gained no pleasure from it.

On our drive back from the lake I noted some most disloyal and Republican sentiments defacing the walls of one dwelling. Mr Wade said it was the work of Pocomaniacs, who held no regard for any authority, let alone God or their Sovereign. Was for stopping the carriage and addressing these loonies on holding such a position but Mr Wade dissuaded me saying he was afraid my discourse might give them cause to *attack* us. So in the evening I obtained the services of Joshua the new coachman, to drive back to this dwelling alone and daub with paint on its door a *proper* sentiment. 'God Save the Queen!' I inscribed to defy them. – I feel my Beloved would have endorsed the action.

This was the date I had arranged for the Wretch Gladstone to receive from me a Letter (addressed from Osborne) expressing my Displeasure in very Round & General Terms on All & Everything he had done the last 3 weeks. If Brown has made sure it was in the Bag the Wretch shd. by now be *Writhing*.

Making Quite Remarkable Use of a Laundry Basket.

Attempting a Novel Form of Aquatic Progress.

Mr W. – who has been remarkably silent on the subject of money during these days we have passed in Port Antonio (so much so that I had started to think his moneys from Boston must have reached him at last) – introduced the matter afresh after 1st Breakfast. Would I, he asked, following my experiences in General Plummett's balloon, be interested in investing in a Trans-Jamaican Balloon Service? I replied that most certainly I would for I had come to see the balloon as the means of transport of the future and such a Service could only be a successful one if guided by a Man of Vision like Mr Wade (Albert I am convinced would have approved my answer). I was about to ask Mr Wade the sum of investment needed when Randy the Cook (a bearer of bad tidings on a previous occasion) came in to us to announce that the General had just perished by falling out of his basket into the hedge-pig pen and that his balloon floated high off in the sky in the directions of Heaven & Cuba. I suggested to Mr Wade we might consider returning to Ocho Rios by carriage and retired to my room with Sir W. Scott.

The drive back to Ocho Rios most *wearisome*. At one point rains had dissolved the road completely and we had to leave our carriages and ford a river on foot – accompanied by a detachment of the Military with whom we had fortuitously met up and who made fresh carriages out of their own supplies on the far side of the river. And thus we arrived at Ocho Rios as though part of some Parade – perhaps 100 men in front of us and twice that number behind I would have estimated. And when their Commander, a giant named Major Ropner, requested permission to camp in the vicinity, Mr Wade most naturally agreed considering both the gt. help they had given us on our journey & the continuing torrential rains which would have made their further progress quite impossible.

Found Colonel M. still exactly as we had left him and ordered that his clothes be changed.

Thursday May 4th

It rained continuously.

There was a List in the paper of *Those Drowned on the Roads of Jamaica Yesterday* – 33 Poor Souls. Also a brief Report that 3 days ago the H. of Commons had supported Mr Gladstone in his proposition to raise the Income Tax so as to meet the Deficiency in the Revenue. – Convinced such an Impertinence need never have happened had I been in the country to dissuade the miserable Wretch from this absurd course. *The Proper Way to balance the Revenue is to be rid of Ireland.*

Being unable to venture out of doors for fear of drowning myself spent the morning having Contests of Tiddlywinks with Miss Biggy & the Midgets. Once when Miss Biggy said she had won I had an outbreak of the Combustibles and after a few minutes Miss Biggy sensibly changed her mind and decided that after all *I* had won.

Passed the afternoon re-reading the paper and revising my List of Things I Don't Like – which I could hardly have looked at in 20 yrs. I crossed out *Mme de Lieven* & *Turtle Soup*, and wrote *Goat Curry*, *Mr Gladstone, Bees & Living in Ireland* in their place. Then I later added *People who Drop Golden Syrup over Me*, & *People who say Nasty Things about Brown.*

Friday May 5th

– Events I found truly unfathomable this day. First, a group of Impertinents threw stones at my good self and Mr Wade when we drove to Ocho Rios in the Sociable (Mr Wade sensibly despatched the lot of them). Then we returned to the house to learn that a group of Tradespersons had called with intent to set fire to the buildings but had been driven off by Miss Biggy and the Midgets pulling faces at them and threatening to pinch them. Finally, I discovered Bishop Kelso blubbering and quivering like some jelly *beneath my bed* and refusing to leave this refuge unless Ned Adam the Strong Man gave him a piggy-back. The man was obviously not just in his cups but quite, quite *mad*. I instructed Mr Wade to remove him and not have him re-admitted to the house.

Passed the remainder of the day pondering these events and wondering what course of action my Dearest Albert would have recommended. Finished up with Sir W. Scott in bed.

A Novel Way of Crossing a River Without Getting Wet.

Executing a Loyal Sentiment.

In the light of the recent unpleasantnesses Mr Wade to-day came to the decision to move his whole Circus to another area of the island, some 70 or so miles along the coast, where he claimed friendship with a Count Diacre,* a sugar planter whose premises he was sure would give adequate shelter to both humans and animals.

Accordingly, he instructed his headman to spend the day packing and encaging the circus with all its etceteras and to start at nightfall for Rattehall in Hanover where we – Mr Wade and myself with Miss Pearly and Randy the Cook – would precede them, leaving immediately by carriage in order to alert Count Diacre of the impending occupation of his lands.

We drove along the coast by Falmouth and Montego Bay until some twenty miles beyond the latter Mr Wade announced we were on the Rattehall Estate. But still further miles we drove through endless sugar fields in which I thought worked gangs of men all chained to one another – perhaps I was mistaken though – before we reached the fair-looking Rattehall Great House.

Such a formidable sight met us upon the house's porch. For there danced and pranced a naked lunatic, beard flying all around him, ranting at a series of terrified blackies who attempted to shelter behind what furnishings they could find. I brushed aside Mr Wade's effort to place his hand over my eyes to shield my susceptibilities from the scene – for I was quite fascinated by the performance. 'Too many times my sight has been sullied with dullness,' I told Mr Wade, 'that when a novelty of sulliment like this happens I wish to drink it in with my eyes to the full.'

Then of a sudden the madman ceased from his folly and, seeing Mr Wade and myself, gallantly raised his hat and bade us welcome. He disappeared inside his premise for a moment and before we had even mounted all the steps of the porch was before us in the flowing robe of an Arab chieftain.

*Count Albert-Philippe Diacre de Liancourt, grandson of Count Louis Diacre de Liancourt who was, acknowledgeably, the son of King Louis XVI of France by the celebrated Duchesse de Montmorency. Count Louis Diacre had fought alongside General Leclerc (husband of Pauline Buonaparte) during the French Army's unsuccessful attempt to put down Dessalines and his Revolutionary forces in Haiti (1799–1804) and had arrived in Jamaica in 1803 to set up trade as a slave importer. So successful was he, with six ships sailing backwards and forwards between Senegal and the West Indies, that he was able to build Rattehall, one of the most splendid of the Great Houses of Jamaica, unique in that every room was provided with a fireplace in which even on the hottest days wood fires blazed. (It was alleged this was because Count Albert-Philippe suffered from the traditional complaint of the Bourbons, that of thin blood.) Surprisingly, this original Rattehall Great House did not burn down in his own lifetime but in his grandson's, fifteen years after Queen Victoria was a guest there.

And such was the substance of my first encounter with Count Diacre. As we sat on his porch over refreshments of his own devising – of a strange minty taste grown from herbs on his own lands, he told us, the receipt known only to himself but coveted by all who ever experienced it – Mr Wade and he discussed how the Circus could be accomodated upon the Estate. Count Diacre said that some of his Slave Quarters could be made available for human members of the Circus and that the animals could either roam loose in the Goat Compound or else he could clear a neighbouring Chapel for their accommodation.

It occurred to me that in his conversation the Count was curiously old-fashioned in many of his views, especially on those of labour and employment. I asked him was it so that the men I had seen working in his fields were really chained together and he agreed most certainly that it was so, and for their own good so that none might ever experience a feeling of loneliness for a lonely man never worked at his best. Even when I remonstrated with him that I believed slavery to have been abolished he simply replied that that might well be so, but that nobody had yet told him. – I was sorry that Colonel Maxwell (who naturally we had brought with us) had still not regained consciousness to be with us for I believe the 2 Gentlemen would have found much in common to agree upon.

But be what he was, Count Diacre gave us handsome rooms (despite the presence of pigs & lizards & hens in some) and five slaves apiece to wait upon us, then bade us rest before the exertions of the evening. – For that night at the Great House he was to hold a Ball (though he lightly referred to it as a 'Jump-Up') to which many of his neighbours were bidden.

Count Diacre.

Randy the Cook.

Pitting One's Wits Against a Red Admiral.

For the occasion, the German Barn in the grounds had been specially decorated and a bonfire lit beside which we practised a native dance called – I think – a *limber*.

The other guests were not the sort I had seen on the Island before, being mostly, like Mr Wade, of an American persuasion, and when I asked one what brought him and his compatriots hence he replied that the soil of Jamaica was especially conducive to the growing of certain crops with which they were experimenting for the greater good of Mankind – more I could not fathom for to me the crops they described sounded like mere grasses.

The womenfolk of these agricultural philanthropists sat around silently sipping Count Diacre's Delicacy, only occasionally gaining an approximate uprightness to dance to the music of a group of poor blackies chained not only to each other but also to their instruments and to the ground below them. And while the night seemed to grow merrier and merrier for some, for me it acquired, with each fresh glass of the Delicacy, an increasing blurredness. I danced finally with a Mr Parrish who told me he had been valet to the Duke of Wellington – though I never heard my beloved Duke kept a Blackie in his service. When he further told me he personally knew the Queen of England and had had to barber and shave her every day for a month I took leave to doubt any and all of his utterances. The fellow, like Count Diacre himself – once again without clothing though singing patriotic ballads – was obviously a madman and I had to ask Mr Wade that we should leave them to each other's company and he could escort me to my room. I further enquired whether Mr Wade had not mistaken some asylum for his friend's house.

My night again made hideous, this time by the noise of the strangling of babes. There must be other ways, I thought, to restrict the population than this which is so searing to the hearing of a person of such sensitive nature as my good self.

The strangling of babes that so plagued me during the past night is explained to me as the noise made by Count Diacre's peacocks who spend the night sleeping in his trees and, when sensing the presence of a mongoose – or any other species of animal unfriendly to them – shriek thus in warning to their mates. I enquired of the Count if he had ever attempted to silence the birds but he replied the pie-case was the only effective silencer and he would order one prepared for my dinner this eve.

Some part of this morning I put aside for making a tour of the Count's estate. Just watching sugar growing I found not to be a v. stimulating activity. More interesting was my discovery of how the Count had solved the problem of gathering the cane growing on the tops of his hills. Carts were built at the top and loaded with the canes and then turned loose, having no alternative but to career down the hillside and smash themselves at the bottom. Then, the cane being sorted from them, the broken pieces of cart were hauled back up the hill, re-built, and the whole process repeated.

This was a method of agriculture, I felt, which could well be practised in the hillier parts of my own kingdom, as well as giving employment to all the out-of-work cart-makers who so frequently petition me for my support. I complimented Count Diacre on his scientific approach to the problem of harvesting hillsides (which would have met with such approval from dear Albert).

Another interesting discovery I made on my Tour of the Estate was a group of 4 young Englishmen – 2 of whom I had noted at table the previous evening – all quite elegantly clothed and gathered round a Scientific Apparatus belching much smoke and a most curious smell. They informed me they were enlisted in Count Diacre's Scheme for Articled Pupils, whereby Persons of Capital in the United Kingdom, in consideration of handing Count Diacre that capital, and coming supplied with their own horse, boy, linen, waterproof cloak and thick-soled boots, received instruction from the Count in the proper running of an Estate. And while waiting for the Count now, for their weekly lesson in Whipping & Cribbage, they had constructed this device for converting sugar to a liquid approximating Scotch whisky which could be distributed amongst the Poor of Hanover (this being the Parish in which we now resided) and they were now industriously engaged in tasting it to discover a flavour which would be appealing to the Poor. I complimented them too upon their Industry and Scientific Approach toward Life.

Upon my journey back toward the Great House I encountered the first sheep I had yet seen upon this island. (Count Diacre keeps them to use as targets on his Sunday shoots.) The pious but stupid and vacant looks on their faces made me in mind of Mr Gladstone, and in my annoyance at having my remembrance so plagued I shouted at the silly creatures and chased them down some hills.

Afterwards, to calm me down, asked Mr Wade to accompany me

An Appropriate Occasion for Establishing Relationships.

The Proper Way to Cook a Parrot Fish at a Picnic.

butterfly-hunting. Saw no very remarkable sight and bagged only one small Yellow Buttertail between us.

Bishop Kelso to dinner and, having consumed an over-sufficiency of Count Diacre's Delicacy sought his usual refuge beneath the dining table before even dinner was commenced, from there making sudden forays toward the bottle-cupboard and once so doing became entangled in Miss Biggy's frocks and in retaliation was pummelled by the Midgets.

The peacock pie – served adorned with the birds' tails – most *tough* – and (what I never thought could come to pass) I actually *asked* for the goat pâté in its place.

Monday May 8th

This day being the anniversary of my dearest Albert's very first gift to me – it was a guinea pig called Noah – I stayed the greater part of the day in bed to muse on other past kindnesses with which he filled my life.

Dressed for dinner and afterwards potted a while with Mr Wade on Count Diacre's snooker table in the yard while the Count accompanied us with sacred music on his organ.

Count Diacre having promised us a picnic we drove off in procession for the sands at Negril this morn, us in the leading coach and 12 carts following behind with the slaves and provisions.

Nearly all the time through sugar fields, past groups of tiny piccaninnies or fishermen carrying their vari-coloured hauls on sticks across their shoulders, until, some 30 miles off, the sands loomed up.

Count Diacre had warned us certain slightly weird persons frequented these sands and indeed, my first sight of them proved his point. For there assembled on the beach to which we visited was such an array of persons lacking any clothing that I looked around for the wreck of some boat thinking only they must be poor castaways just landed. Some dozen of them, brown and long-bearded the men, long-haired and almost black the women, played upon musical instruments – 5 naked violinists of the male sex, 3 cellist ladies also lacking in any cover, and 1 unprotected indeterminate upon the double bass. To their sounds – for I could not grace the noise with the name of music – the other unclothed castaways gyrated – again in a way that I had never seen at Balls, in twos and threes closely to one another, more like clockwork animals than humans. Half in shock, half in fascination, I watched the scene with Mr Wade and Miss Biggy the Fat Lady, while Count Diacre organised his slaves in the setting up of tables and the laying-out of foodstuffs. We ate well of Kingfish and freshwater Shrimp and afterward the Count approached one of the bearded nudies and after a long negotiation with the man returned to our table with a small package the contents of which he said, when made into a compact roll and smoked like a cigarette, proved a most efficacious tonic-medicine in these parts.

After some few puffs at one I felt most elated and any pains I or my body might have been harbouring completely disappeared. Danced with one of the long-locked blackies then felt a most urgent desire to rush up and down the beach crying and flapping my arms like the wings of a hen-bird. Continued thus for some hours – so Mr Wade informed me later but I had little recollection of it except of waking up in my own bed at Count Diacre's Great House and feeling afuzz in my head and body.

Mr Wade with the sad news that most of his Clowns have perished in the storm of last night, some washed away to sea, some hit by lightening, some flattened by falling boulders. But praise be to God 3 have survived.

After this sad start to a day arranged to be driven by Count Diacre's tipsy coachman to do the marketing in Montego. And on our way we (for Miss Pearly was by my side with all her baskets) passed such a remarkable spectacle. – Hundreds & hundreds of blackies in long white nightgowns making a procession of themselves in the sea off Hopewell Beach. It was a Baptism of persons of the Baptist persuasion, Miss Pearly explained to me, and the person furthest out in the sea – little more than his head and the tops of his shoulders above the water level – was the priest immersing, one by one, both old and new members of his congregation. – Most re-appearing almost instantly after their immersion, but some, I noted, not, and being swept out to sea pursued fruitlessly by a boatman – for none of them, Miss Pearly assured me, had ever mastered the arts of Floating & Stroking which was the reason their companions made no move to rescue them. And the priest, she further explained, was anchored to the seabed

Further Exercises in Losing One's Weight While Retaining One's Dignity.

Enjoying a Smoke on the Sands.

for fear he should drift away, and as a further safeguard for his longevity was attended by two top-hatted Elders of the Church who would right him – for he was a frail old man much given to Toppling – whenever any wave of exceptional height should overcome him.

It struck me as an extremely dangerous profession, that of a Baptist priest; indeed, being a Baptist at all, full of hazard. I opined that the Church lost just as many members as it gained through this habit of immersion. The *font*, such as my own dear children were Christened in when they were received into *my* Church, is obviously a most sensible and life-saving invention and its inventor, I trust, was once suitably honoured.

The Market at Montego hot and crowded, and Count Diacre's Shopping List not at all easy to comply with. 1 doz qts of Black Betty (but not to pay more than $4\frac{1}{4}$d a qt.), 6 Heaps of Peppers, 2 medium-sized Turtles, 1 Box Good Leaches, 2 lbs Gunpowder, 1 doz Burning Sticks, and 20 lbs of such meat as was available. Complained to the market person that to charge 5d per lb for Goats' Flesh was exorbitant, and settled for $4\frac{1}{2}$d worth of Mixed Shad and Mackerel, and 6 Small Goats (11d each, a much more reasonable price).

Mr Wade, when we returned, with the news that 1 of the Surviving Clowns had perished by falling off the shoulders of his fellows & striking his head against a milestone. And these 2 others, so saddened by this event, had taken refuge in a Chapel at Sandy Bay and were threatening to become Holy Men.

Thursday May 11th

This a.m. Mr Wade broke to me the sad information that Ned Allen the Strong Man had slipped over a banana skin & inflicted such injuries to himself that Mr W. had felt it kinder to have him put down.

Friday May 12th

Mr Wade said at breakfast to-day that in the light of his recent severe losses his best plan would be to make an expedition to the neighbouring island of Haiti where not only could he replenish his Clowns, but also, with the advice of Mr Ponce, his Livery Stable Master, purchase a number of horses to replace those which had met with Stumbling Accidents of late and which were needed to train for Miss Biggy the Fat Lady to ride in the Ring.

He asked, on account of his moneys from Boston still being mysteriously overdue, if I would finance and join them on this Expedition to Haiti.

– I recollected that one of my last dull duties before leaving England had been to receive, at the behest of Earl Granville, the Minister Plenipotentiary of this Black Republic, a General Brice whose collar and uniform had been so covered in gold lace and feathers his face was barely discernible. But I refrained from mentioning the encounter to Mr Wade. In the guise of Mrs King I replied simply that I should be honoured to accompany him and Mr Ponce upon any equestrian mission to any country at any time.

Whereupon Mr Wade bid me to be ready in two hours' time when the sloop he had chartered to take us on our journey would depart.

I directed Miss Pearly to pack for us and two hours later we were upon the seas again.

A most uncomfortable 24 hours. The boat did much rocking, and I much writhing and Mr Ponce went overboard – an inconsiderate action on his part I complained to Mr Wade for he had in his pocket at the time the copy of Mr Wordsworth's poems I had lent him for his improvement.

Another new country. Very obviously not Mine in that nobody appears to be speaking or understanding English – if only these backward peoples could understand the benefits to be derived from acquiring a language that *proper* people know.

Immediately upon our disembarking Mr Wade obtained the services of a horse and cabriolet with driver and directed the latter to take us to the rendez-vous he had arranged with his horse-dealer some way up the incline between the town of Port-au-Prince and the hill resort of Petionville. This turned out to be a handsome mansion called La Vieille Maison, and Monsieur Sam, the horse-dealer, although of an Indian colour and with a

Pausing to Marvel at a Mass Baptism.

Taking an Advanced Course in Equestrianism.

humped back and total lack of hair, a person of intelligence in that he had obviously put aside a period of his life to attempt a command of English. He paraded his horses (ridden by members of the Petionville Hunt) in front of us, and Mr Wade pleased me by referring to my judgment upon numerous occasions. – How uplifting to be in the company of a person of such innate Good Taste.

Having made our purchases – some 18 healthy beasts each reckoned strong enough to bear Miss Biggy the Fat Lady performing on its back – and having requested that they be delivered to our sloop we started our way back to Port-au-Prince. Passing the Hubert Hobbyhorse Race Course on our route, Monsieur Sam, espying some of his servants amongst the racegoers, paused briefly to shoot two of them – a discipline I congratulated him on maintaining in these lax times; and then we proceeded for luncheon to the seaside premises of a certain Madame Evelyne – a lady, Monsieur Sam, explained to us, of charitable nature who provided employment for poor girls of the town who lacked qualifications to work in the more hide-bound business premises. Monsieur Sam ordered us all bowls of oysters and some chilled white wines, then he and Mr Wade asked permission to take leave of me briefly while they discussed a business matter with Madame Evelyne. I did not demur even though I realised this would create the first occasion during my trip that I would be without a *man* by my side. And nor need I have worried on this account for while the 2 Gentlemen were absent there were many others who came up to me to make my acquaintance, and even some who, presumably taking pity on my lonely state, approached offering financial contributions toward my well-being – a quaint local custom I thought, and in return for the silver pieces they proferred I graciously donated to each of them one of the flowers I had had Miss Pearly pick for me outside La Vieille Maison earlier in the morning. Imagine then my surprise when the reaction of one fellow to my generosity was to bite the flower into two halves, throw them upon the floor and stamp on them with his feet. Imagine my further surprise with what happened next. The fellow's companion, a milder man, remonstrated with him over his behaviour whereupon the fellow delivered him with a mighty punch in the stomach which sent him sprawling half-way across the room. And then pandemonium broke loose. While the band continued to play in one corner and a number of couples continued to dance by them everyone else in the place seemed concerned with hitting everyone else. Bottles were being broke, furniture flying, people falling down like skittle-pins. I had never known such excitement. To defend myself and Miss Pearly at one point I even had to get out of my chair and lift it to smash over the head of some lewd fellow. And then as suddenly as this pandemonium had started it ceased as into the midst of the room came, blowing whistles and shouting orders, a whole squadron of uniformed persons. Some few of the original inmates of the room jumped into the sea and swam off but the rest of us were hustled out into the street and thrown into a large covered cart, Miss Pearly still beside me though now in an avalanche of tears, myself enjoying the experience immensely.

But what, I wondered as we were driven off, had become of Mr Wade and Monsieur Sam? Had they been so intent upon their business with Madame Evelyne they had remained undisturbed by the whole commotion? And now where was I going? After a bare ten minutes I found out, as we were herded out of the cart and pushed into a plain brick building the interior of which was partitioned by a series of strong bars running from floor to ceiling and wall to wall. We were in prison. What should I do now? Demand the British Consul? – But he might recognise me and that would be the end of my masquerade. No. I had to go through with this thing, trusting in God, as Mrs King.

I dare say had they known who was gracing their cells that night the food we were given might have been better, but at least *gruel* made a change from goat. I was attemping to convey to our gaoler my wish to learn from the chef the receipt for this delicious tasting mess when who should appear but Mr Wade in the company of a person in the grandest uniform I had ever seen. There were profuse apologies from this latter over my predicament and heartfelt expressions of regret from Mr Wade that his business had detained him during the late disturbance. Then the door of our cell was unlocked and I was escorted out of the building, and Mr Wade and his splendid-uniformed companion – the chief Policeman of Port-au-Prince it developed – escorted me out of the house of confinement.

We had, through this dalliance of mine, Mr Wade explained, missed the time of sailing of our sloop and so would need to spend the night in town but kinsmen of Monsieur Sam ran a fine hostelry and to that we now repaired. The Grand Hotel Sam turned out to be not just a fine establishment but also architecturally quite amazing. It was as though some half dozen lunatics had been given charge to build the place and each proceeded all over it with his own style to the total disregard of the style of his fellows. – The end look, all in pierced wood and tin being not unlike a piece of poor Maud's crochet-work. There was a Chamberlain dressed all in white to greet us upon the verandah of the place but before we could mount the dozen steps to reach his side we were surrounded by persons who suddenly emerged from down trees and behind bushes to opportune us with their

Coping with Some Lewd Fellows During a Pandemonium.

Entering into the Spirit of a Carnival.

wares – brightly-coloured paintings of giraffes and zebras, statues in wood of snakes and hens. I would have dallied in inspection of their items but Mr Wade thrust the exhibitors aside impatiently and bade me mount the steps before him. The Chamberlain profuse with words of welcome so that I believed he must know my true identity but Mr Wade explains the man speaks thus to everyone. A Ball appeared to be taking place beyond the verandah, but the dancing of a kind I had never before seen – more like to gymnastics than the movements which grace my Ballrooms. Prompted by Mr Wade I was soon in the midst of it, copying the other dancers, my arms twirling over my head, my lower limbs taking as much exercise as any sprinter.

Suddenly in the midst of the dancing a shriek from outside. Everyone rushes out on to the verandah which overlooks a small ornamental lake – though there is but an inch or 2 of water at its base there also on its bottom lies Bishop Kelso! Most opine that he is dead which I quickly disabuse them of through the simple expedient of banging two bottles together thus producing a miraculous revival. We asked him how he came to be in Haiti and he replied bafflingly that it was nothing to do with his having been convicted for preaching without a licence. I really do find the Bishop's behaviour *most* extraordinary.

Early to-day to watch the Carnival in the town and for Mr Wade to choose some Clowns from it. It is a long procession of blackies dancing through the streets banging on drums and making noise from bamboo sticks. Some wearing top hats and lawyers' suitings, some in tiger masks with peacock tails, but I preferred most the party all of whom were dressed as *me* – 40 or 50 Queens a-whooping and a-whirling. It is a thought I should pass on to the good D. of Norfolk for the next Procession of mine he organises.

Later, Mr Wade, saying he had been much impressed with my dancing at the hotel last night, enters me for a Marathon Meringue Contest where I dance four hours without cease and find a way of winning by putting my foot out when other dancers pass by so causing them to collide with the ground. My Prize, a small black pig.

Contorting Oneself While Attempting a Local Dance.

Tuesday May 16th

After breakfast Mr Wade declared his sloop was ready for sailing and that we should board it for our return trip to Montego Bay in Jamaica.

I could not understand where were all the horses that Mr Wade had bought until I visited my cabin and found 6 of them standing at their ease tethered to my towel rails and eating bran out of my bath. – Mr Wade quite dumb-founded when I told him; then, on his way to study the spectacle, discovered *12* horses in *his* cabin. It must, he said, be a Haitian joke perpetrated by his new Clowns. I told him I did not think Haitian Jokes were very amusing jokes and asked if he would please have his live-stock removed at any rate from *my* cabin and the cabin cleansed and made available for my occupation.

Spent the rest of the day once we were at sea trying to take my mind off the roll of the boat and wondering whether perhaps Haitian Jokes were a *little* bit amusing & making up some of my own like Putting Pigs in Mr Gladstone's Dressing Room or Filling Mr Gladstone's Bed with Crabs. All of *my* Jokes struck me as being *very* amusing and when I told them to Miss Pearly she also said they were.

Wednesday May 17th

Landed at Montego in time for tea (toast with Solomon Grundy at Miss Delisser's Tea-Rooms) and drove straight by carriage to Rattehall. Count Diacre well pleased to see us back & *most* happy with the Tick Powders & bars of Washing-Soap I had brought him (for there was, when we left, a great dearth of these commodities upon the island).

Two different sorts of Goat Curry for dinner, followed by snooker and sacred tunes. I really do feel being back here at Rattehall is just like *Coming Home* and complimented the Count – though he was not a little merry from his Delicacy – on his ability as a Host.

All day jerking with the hiccoughs. My good self nor anyone could do anything about it, except opine I must have overeaten of Miss Delisser's Solomon Grundy. Toward evening Count Diacre fed me a little laudanum and when I awoke at 11 p.m. I was myself again. A note from Mr Wade saying he had gone pig-hunting in the hills.

Such sadness. Count Diacre at breakfast opined – and he apologised for having forgot to mention it the previous night – that my good, true Col. M. who has been laid in a back billiards room all this time beneath the Count's cue rack, is dead; and in fact, judging from the scents emanating from his locality, has most probably been dead these last four weeks. Much, *much* saddened by this news, for though I had noted that the Col. had not moved at all those four weeks I had thought it was but a temporary weariness on his part.

Accordingly I requested the Count to make arrangements for the Col's burial. The Count recommended the churchyard of Lucea some 10 miles distant where, he assured me, many other decent people lay buried. And further, he said, seeing that the Col. was a Military man he would alert the Military at Fort Charlotte nearby to provide a proper escort and instruct the populace to line the streets in a fitting grieving manner. And to convey the Col. to this engagement the Count submitted we should convert one of the hillside sugar trucks into a funeral bier which could be suitably decorated by the Count's constructors and drawn to Lucea by 20 of his strongest slaves.

All this came to pass within a matter of hours. Women from the slave quarters collected flowers with which wreaths were made and lain on top of Colonel Maxwell's coffin on the bier, and the procession solemnly formed up at the top of Count Diacre's drive outside Rattehall Great House, the bier in front, Bishop Kelso following on horseback with his bottle-bearers (thinly disguised as bell-ringers) alongside, the rest of us on foot behind. Solemn we were and yet within a moment of our moving off there was a wild pandemonium. For no-one had given thought that the great bier

Teaching the Young a Decent British Game.

An Unanticipated Occurrence at a Dear Friend's Funeral.

should have, on this slope, been *constrained* by the 20 slaves *from behind* and not pulled by them *in advance*. As soon as they put it in movement the great bier simply rolled over them and – like its fellows bearing canes on Count Diacre's hillsides – careered down the drive ending up embedded in the cotton tree beside the Slave Hospital. There was an awful silence (except for the moaning of those careless enough to be run over by the runaway bier), and then from the ruins of the bier rose a grotesque – but most welcome – figure, that of my dear Col Maxwell clothed in the red calico night-shirt that had been thought appropriate for his stay in Lucea and he in a strident tone demanding to know the occasion of this chaos.

Bishop Kelso at this moment fell off his horse in what he later lyingly described as a faint: the unwounded blackies and their fellows ran off into the cane-fields jabbering wildly: but I was totally, completely overjoyed to see my good old Colonel M. so obviously alive and risen from the dead.

Count Diacre promptly apologised to me for diagnosing the Colonel's condition as Dead and explained that we had to thank the severity of the collision we had just witnessed for jarring the Col's inert body into life again.

Colonel Maxwell, still with no understanding of what had happened or why he was garbed in a scarlet night-dress, or where he was (for his accident had occurred at Ocho Rios), seemed infinitely relieved to catch sight of my good self as, escorted by Count Diacre, I advanced down the drive toward him. I introduced him to the Count, told him I would explain all later but that in the meantime he should accompany us to the dining table of Ratte-hall for assuredly, after 4 weeks of fasting, he must have an impressive hunger. And while a luncheon was arranged for the Col., Count Diacre set about making his arrangements so that the grieving populace and Military Escort waiting at Lucea should not be disappointed by the postponement of the Colonel's trip into their midst. He organised that one of the poor blackies rolled over by the runaway bier should be sent to them as a substitution.

How truly pleased I am to have Colonel M. back again! As he has no know-ledge at all of the events of the last month I have spent some hours reading from my Diary to him. What has concerned him most deeply has been the sums of money I had paid to Mr Wade, and later in the day, after Mr Wade had returned from his pig-hunt in the hills, and after his surprise at seeing Colonel M. so revived had diminished, I overheard an angry exchange between the 2 Gentlemen. Later still the Col. came to report to me that he had caused Mr Wade to admit he had no possible way of repaying the sums I had advanced to him – that all the stories Mr W. had given me, of moneys he was expecting from the United States, were mere fabrications; and that further, the great spate of deaths amongst the Circus performers had all been engineered by Mr W. to avoid paying the poor persons their due salaries; and that in these circumstances Colonel M. had caused Mr W. to sign a document making over to my good self the Title to his Circus – that being Mr W's only Asset.

I was greatly surprised by this information for Mr Wade had seemed all along to me such a *Gentleman*. To find myself so *used* by him moved me exceedingly and I asked to spend the rest of the day by myself.

I looked at the inventory Col. M. had given me of the Circus and it was a most uninspiring Document:

1 Tent with Some Poles & Some Ropes
3 (three) Clowns (1 with 1 leg only)
2 (two) Aerialists (1 leg between the 2)
1 Fat Lady
1 Strong Man
2 (two) Midgets
Remains of 2 Others
Assorted Mechanical Contraptions
12 Cages on Some Wheels
14 Horses
1 Lion
2 Boxes Fire-eating equipment
1 (one) Elephant (Dead)

Putting a Fine Feat of Engineering to Enjoyable Use.

Perfecting One's Drive.

I reached my room to find a most beautiful bunch of Stinkwort & Blue Belchflowers, to which was attached a note in Mr Wade's hand. He craved my forgiveness for what he was afraid I might consider his duplicity and gave the very commendable explanation that it was only because he could conceive no other way to have my companionship for so long – which companionship was what he had come to value most in all the world. He apologised for his emotions prevailing so over his integrity and commonsense, and said he was repairing immediately to the African continent where, as condonance for his behaviour he planned to pass the rest of his life converting the natives there to a better way of life by lecturing them and imbuing them with the knowledge of my good and gentle nature.

Poor Mr Wade! *He* to Africa* because of me and my good and gentle nature, and *I* left with his Circus. What good, I pondered, could beloved Albert have worked with such a toy.

The events of the day before have taken their toll of my emotions and I have passed all the day on my bed Pondering & Musing. Oh poor Mr Wade to whom most of my Ponders & Muses were devoted.

Also I have been reading letters & cards from the children which had collected for me in my absence and Count Diacre had to-day remembered came. Vicky says that Fritz has taken France and would I like any of it. Alex says that Bertie is smoking less but coughing more and that Mr Gladstone is wearing his arm in a sling in a diabolical move to engender sympathy for himself and his inept policies. And Helena is with child again.

Throughout the day I have heard sounds of Count Diacre in great ill-humour, and Miss Pearly has appraised me it is because some hundreds of men† have camped on his land with instruction from the Governor to

*In fact, Arnold Wade went to South America. By the end of 1871 he was proprietor of the Wade Novelty Hat Co. of Buenos Aires, which his descendants still run. In correspondence with them it is clear that they are aware of their ancestor's circus past but – up until now – ignorant of the period that Queen Victoria passed in his company. He died in 1901 and is buried in Buenos Aires.

†These were, of course, the ever-protective British Naval force – presumably in such great numbers owing to the dangerously isolated position of Rattehall. The quite unnecessary bridge they constructed over the Maggotty River at this point is still referred to as Irish Bridge.

make a bridge over it where no bridge has ever been before and no bridge is needed. Looking out from my verandah I was able to see them all, like so many plaguey Irish persons at work, the one half seated on their spades and brewing tea, the others engaged in discussion and they and their womenfolk pummelling each other on the ground. I heard the Count as the day proceeded raise his voice higher and higher in condemnation of the men's existence, and shout the Governor was a Fop & Silly man, not worthy of his high position.

Count Diacre's foul humour continued all the morning. Should he come upon some house-slave with but half a smile upon his face, or should he hear one hum – however quietly – some piece of tune, it would cause the Count to snarl, to run berserk, to seize the hapless fellow and demand by what right he had to be happy while meant to be at work for him.

But by eventide he had become calmed. He had passed the afternoon, he said, in the company of the new clowns, inciting them to ride his billy-goats and – so mounted – to charge the ranks of the plaguey Irish bridge-builders at the bottom of his drive, while he retired to watch through his spy-glass the havoc that this manoeuvre caused. Indeed, so good was his mood that when before dinner 2 of his field-slaves were brought before him accused of *Nibbling* – of having been discovered eating a piece of the raw cane they were engaged in cutting – instead of sentencing them to attend Wednesday Whippings as punishment, he bade them stay by us and asked solicitously concerning their conditions of employment and satisfied himself that their *Nibbling* had been occasioned by pleasure and not by hunger. I much admired the Count's benevolence at this moment.

My *Birthday*! (– and may the Good God bless & Preserve me for *many* more). Cards from Bertie and Louise, a scarf and mittens from Eddy & George, and Randy the Cook had decorated the Jerk Pork & Eggs served for my breakfast with some pretty little pieces of funny-smelling green grass.

A Way of Livening Up a Party at a Waterfall.

Imagining a Happy Future as a Tradesperson.

Count Diacre – kind, *considerate* man that he is (despite his bouts of nakedness) had arranged a luncheon party for me on the top of Drivers Falls – the tables, chairs & Guests actually a foot deep in the waters at the top of the Waters. Those members of the Circus who survived the goat curry of yesterday are present – except the Midgets not for long as they do not possess sufficient weight to prevent themselves being swept over the edge when I give them a playful push.

To bring back a smile to people's faces at this event I do one of my Swings, from one side of the river to *nearly* the other, unfortunately landing on the Midgets' mother who displays great fortitude by not complaining at all before she expires. – How gracious is God's will that they should all go together. Count Diacre congratulates me on my high-spiritedness but I am in a black humour on account my landing on the old crone has crushed the pink flower Randy the Cook gave me – but then the Count soothes me by talking of further delights he has arranged for me on this evening.

[*Editor's Note:* two pages of the original Diary are missing at this point. From what follows it seems most likely they would have described the Queen's progress back to Rattehall in the face of a gale of ever-increasing force, and her discovery there of the Circus tent erected on the grass in front of the Great House – that presumably being the 'further delight' that Count Diacre had organized for her.]

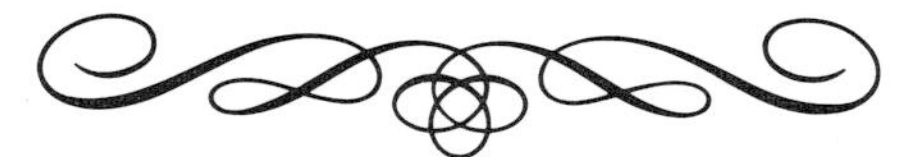

The scene as we entered the Great Tent – more *blown* into it by the force of the tearing wind and rain than transported voluntarily by our feet – was a *Bedlam.* The plaguey Irish bridge-builders had been brought in to act as audience and so there were they and their womenfolk singing and pummelling each other all over the ground. And upon their writhing bodies were falling aerialists at a most alarming rate. In one corner stood two men apparently on fire. In another, six apparently being mauled by the lion I recognised as the naughty one who had consumed dear Maud. The Count apologised to me that the performers – slaves of his he had instructed that morning to become proficient in the arts of the Circus – were showing themselves so woefully inefficient. But the rest of what the good man had to say was interrupted as the noise of the winds blowing outside increased to a most piercing scream and the elements suddenly broke into and filled the great tent so that like a great balloon it started to rise off the ground – our good selves too. And so I suddenly found I was floating, parted from the Count, blown around in the atmosphere like a common Autumn leaf and mingling with plaguey Irish and animals alike – an experience totally beyond the ken of any of my previous aerial activities. One moment I was transported upon my back, the next I was like a ball, and the next after that I was upside downwards and blowing sideways. It was confusing.

Then, as suddenly as it had sprung up, this mighty wind which carried all of us at its mercy abated. I and everybody else, and the animals and trees which floated in the sky, started falling downwards. My own fall – superior to that of many others through my knowledge of *plummeting* – being broken by the top boughs of a mango tree – a fruit I had not previously much cared for – where I sat until those who I have earlier described as the plaguey Irish came seeking me, then formed a great pyramid of their bodies and carried me down over it. Their surprising concern for my well-being made me relent for several minutes my attitude toward their country. (But *not* toward the wretch Gladstone).

It was, I opined to Count Diacre over the goat-curry at dinner, one of the most remarkable birthdays I had passed.

Reading the report in to-day's newspaper of how yesterday the *Queen's* Birthday was celebrated on this island – with a public Holiday, and gun salutes from the ships at Port Royal *and* from the Military at each fort on land – brought home to me, as nothing else has done so far, the nature of my position.

To continue in my present circumstance leading this *gadabout* life as owner of a Circus – albeit a Circus now without performers – or to return to my Family & Responsibilities at home. And when I asked how beloved Albert would have ordered it I realised no other alternative was possible but the latter. And oh, how I would like to feel the scents of the Highlands again and be rid of the Bees who still pester my body here, how I should like to be driving with honest Brown at my side, how I should like to experience a *sausage* again, or Spotted Dick with *proper* custard – how I really long for everything at home again, except to have the miserable pompous Gladstone in my company.

Accordingly, this being my thinking, I took counsel of my dear Colonel

Experiencing a High Wind in Jamaica.

M. who assured me that on the morrow was a packet leaving from Montego Bay for Liverpool via New York, and which if he left my presence now to see its Captain he was sure he could gain accommodation on. I concurred with him, directing that he should book berths also for Miss Pearly and Randy the Cook.

Then, as the Col. departed on his mission, I commenced to write a letter to dear mad Count Diacre commending him for the hospitality he had given and the courtesies he had shown me, enjoining him to make what use he wished of the poor beasts who were the survivors of my Circus, and all the mechanical contrivances that had survived my attempts to exercise upon them.

I left the letter in a servant's keeping so the Count could not open it till after we had gone, and that night at dinner I was my most charming to him, passing him the salt before he even asked for it, & afterward let him beat me *three* times at Cribbage which made him *most* benign.

It was with the most confused of feelings that, while Count Diacre was occupied in his cane-fields giving instruction in Flogging & Abuse to his Articled Pupils that my good self and Col. Maxwell, with Miss Pearly & Randy the Cook, drove off to Montego to catch the packet* to New York & England. And oh, England! Soon to be in Frogmore again! Soon to see my faithful Brown (surely cured of his bashfulness by now) again! And the children!

Before boarding spent 2 hrs in the stores of Montego – having been told they were better value than those of Sandy Bay or Hopewell – purchasing Gifts to take back to all.

For Vicky & Fritz, a Stuffed Mongoose. For Bertie & Alix, 12 Table-mats (with humorous Pictures of Slaves being Scourged & Flogged); for Alice & Louis, 6 Table-mats (plain); for Affie, 1 Carving of a man with a big Thing for Cracking Nuts; for Helena & Louise & Beatrice, jars of Solomon Grundy paste; for Arthur, 1 box Cigars; and for Brown (as he prefers his Liquids)

*Going by the Shipping Movements column of the *Daily Gleaner* of this date, this would have had to have been the U.S. vessel *Andrew Polk*. A check with the records of the Schlumberger Line – to which the vessel belonged – shows that this ship put in at Havana on its way to New York, and then spent two weeks in New York undergoing repairs to a faulty rudder. This also bears out the date of the Queen's established re-appearance at Balmoral on 30 June – even if it does leave one speculating how she passed those two weeks in New York.

1 bott. Coconut Milk. For all the g'children I bought duty-free crayons & Painting Sets (and for the wretch Gladstone† Absolutely Nothing), and all together I spent 16 shillings.

I boarded the packet exhausted from this buying and retired straight to my Accommodation.

†The Prime Minister eventually visited the Queen at Balmoral on 20 July. At the meeting neither party apparently made any reference to the Queen's absence but the Queen wrote to her eldest daughter shortly afterwards:

'. . . come to explain the Revisions to his ridiculous Match Tax to me, the wretched man unnaturally nervous – nor did I ask him to be seated at any time – hardly looking me in the face for fear, I suspect, it might not even be me but one of the Browns as me and in that event not knowing what his stand shd. be.

'I took the gtest. pleasure in making him *squirm* as much as possible, asking him pointedly if he did not find me looking much improved from when he lasted visited me *one month ago* (when I was not here!); and asking him if he had yet considered an answer to the question I had put him at that time – then pretending much offence that he failed to remember the subject of my question . . .'

In the context of the Queen's absence abroad the contents of this letter which has for so long baffled historians now of course makes complete sense.

Negotiating an Object During the Return Voyage.

Editor's Postscript

What staggered me most when I first read extracts from this Diary was – if it was genuine – the size of the conspiracy which must have existed to keep the public from knowing of Queen Victoria's absence from the United Kingdom. Neither at the time, nor for nearly 100 years, did any word of it become public knowledge. I was equally impressed by the extraordinary lengths to which the conspirators must have gone. Gladstone writing his weekly letters to a Queen he knew wasn't there and pretending to receive replies which he knew had never been sent to him. Sir William Jenner and his assistant Dr James Barracough making up and issuing their totally false medical bulletins. John Brown's relatives taking it in turns to dress up and impersonate the Queen at those small public functions – attending church from Balmoral, laying the stone of the new College at Aberdeen. Could it really ever have been John Brown or Hamish Brown so garbed? Or was it always Patsy? The mind completely boggles at the thought of John, perhaps not totally temperate, dressed in a bonnet and skirt of the Queen and receiving his – and her – arch-enemy Mr Gladstone. And then all those Naval officers and seamen lurking in the Jamaican undergrowth, sometimes disguised as butterfly-collectors, sometimes as undertakers, guarding their Queen from they knew not what – and yet their presence never to be detected by her.

Above all, I think one has to admire the industry of Princess Beatrice who twenty years later edited all her mother's Diaries (frequently by throwing the original pages into the fire and writing totally new and – what she considered – more *proper* entries) and who, faced with a total three-month blank in these Diaries, coincident with the period her mother was in Jamaica, invented a series of events in her mother's life at Osborne and Balmoral of such monumental dullness and lifelessness that one just *has* to suspect them of not being real.

If one asks *why* the reason for this great cover-up I can only submit that the Establishment, meaning Gladstone's men in the first instance, felt that the whole fabric of Victorian Society would crumble if it became common knowledge that the symbol of it all, the Queen, was a mere mortal like anyone else and capable of leading a mere mortal's existence, fraternizing with circus proprietors, talking with clowns, above all *enjoying* herself. That had to be the reason for the plot of silence initially. While incredibility had to be the subsequent reason, during all those years after the Queen died.

Who would be willing to believe an old salt who claimed that forty years earlier he and forty mates had had to dress up as undertakers in a Jamaican forest in order to prevent Queen Victoria from being kidnapped?

The alternative, of course, is that the Diary was not genuine. I had many doubts about it from the start. However, after publication of the extracts in the *Observer* I was approached by the Inter-Continental hotel group to decorate a Queen Victoria dining-room they had suddenly decided to create in their new hotel at Ocho Rios. And I was also approached by some Jamaican charities to display new paintings of the Queen in Jamaica on their behalf. It seemed to be in my own interests to get the Diary substantiated as quickly as possible.

My initial efforts to do this were quite disastrous. I looked up Braborough in *Debrett* and there was no one of such a name. I asked a friend to check on the address he had given the *Observer* and it turned out to be that of a hot-dog stand in the middle of a road in Coral Gables, Miami, – not even a *Mr* Braborough running it.

I asked another friend to apply to the Royal Archivist at Windsor concerning the time the Queen was meant to have been in Jamaica. There was ample proof, replied the archivist, from the Queen's Journal, and from her public appearances during that time that she must have been at Osborne and Balmoral. I looked at every possible Memoir of the time seeking some clue, Gladstone's Letters, the Ponsonby Letters, the Kronberg Letters, the Queen's Letters and Journal – not even a clue to a clue in any of them.

I did as much checking as possible on the Queen's alleged companions during her trip, Lt-Colonel Augustus Crosbie Maxwell and Mrs Maud Beswick. Such a Maxwell appeared sixteen times in the Court Circular between 1871 and 1895 when he died, 'mourned by all', at his home West Green House in Hartley Whitney, Hampshire. More telling, from the records of Somerset House, was the existence of Maud Beswick who died of 'tropical diseases' in 1871 – the year she was consumed by lions in Jamaica. The information was encouraging but it still didn't mean that the Mrs King in whose company the two were had been Queen Victoria.

I tried the family of Sir John Peter Grant, Governor of Jamaica during Queen Victoria's alleged visit. At Staddledbridge in Yorkshire where they lived they could produce no records at all of their ancestor and referred me to a cousin who in the twenties had upped and gone with most of the family possessions to start life as a sheep-farmer in New Zealand – I kept that one for if all else failed.

Finally, with the realization I was getting nowhere, I thought maybe the answer had to lie in Jamaica.

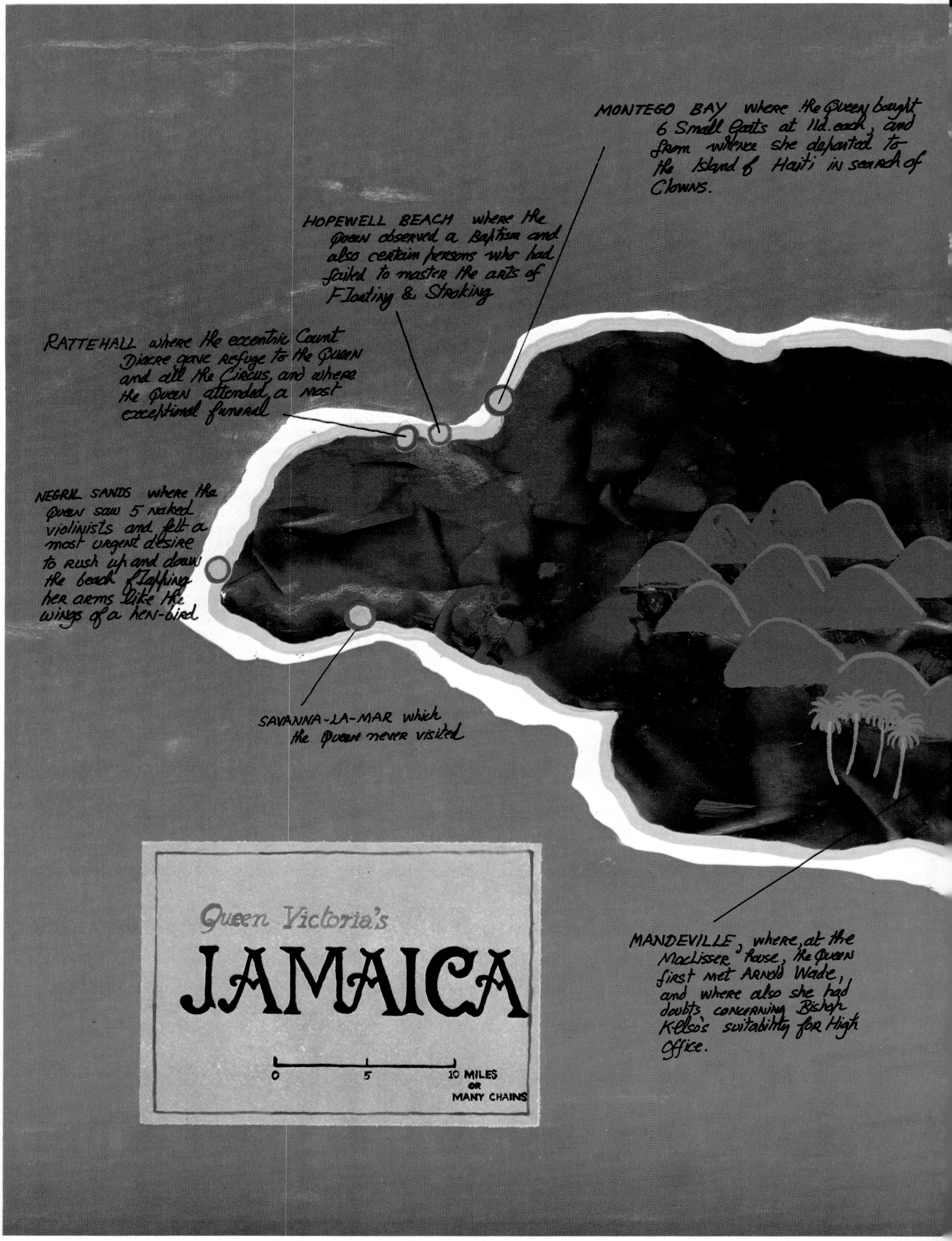

MONTEGO BAY where the Queen bought 6 Small Goats at 11d. each, and from whence she departed to the Island of Haiti in search of Clowns.

HOPEWELL BEACH where the Queen observed a Baptism and also certain persons who had failed to master the arts of Floating & Stroking

RATTEHALL where the eccentric Count Diacre gave Refuge to the Queen and all the Circus, and where the Queen attended a most exceptional funeral

NEGRIL SANDS where the Queen saw 5 naked violinists and felt a most urgent desire to rush up and down the beach flapping her arms like the wings of a hen-bird

SAVANNA-LA-MAR which the Queen never visited

Queen Victoria's

JAMAICA

0 5 10 MILES OR MANY CHAINS

MANDEVILLE, where, at the MacLisser house, the Queen first met Arnold Wade, and where also she had doubts concerning Bishop Kelso's suitability for High Office.

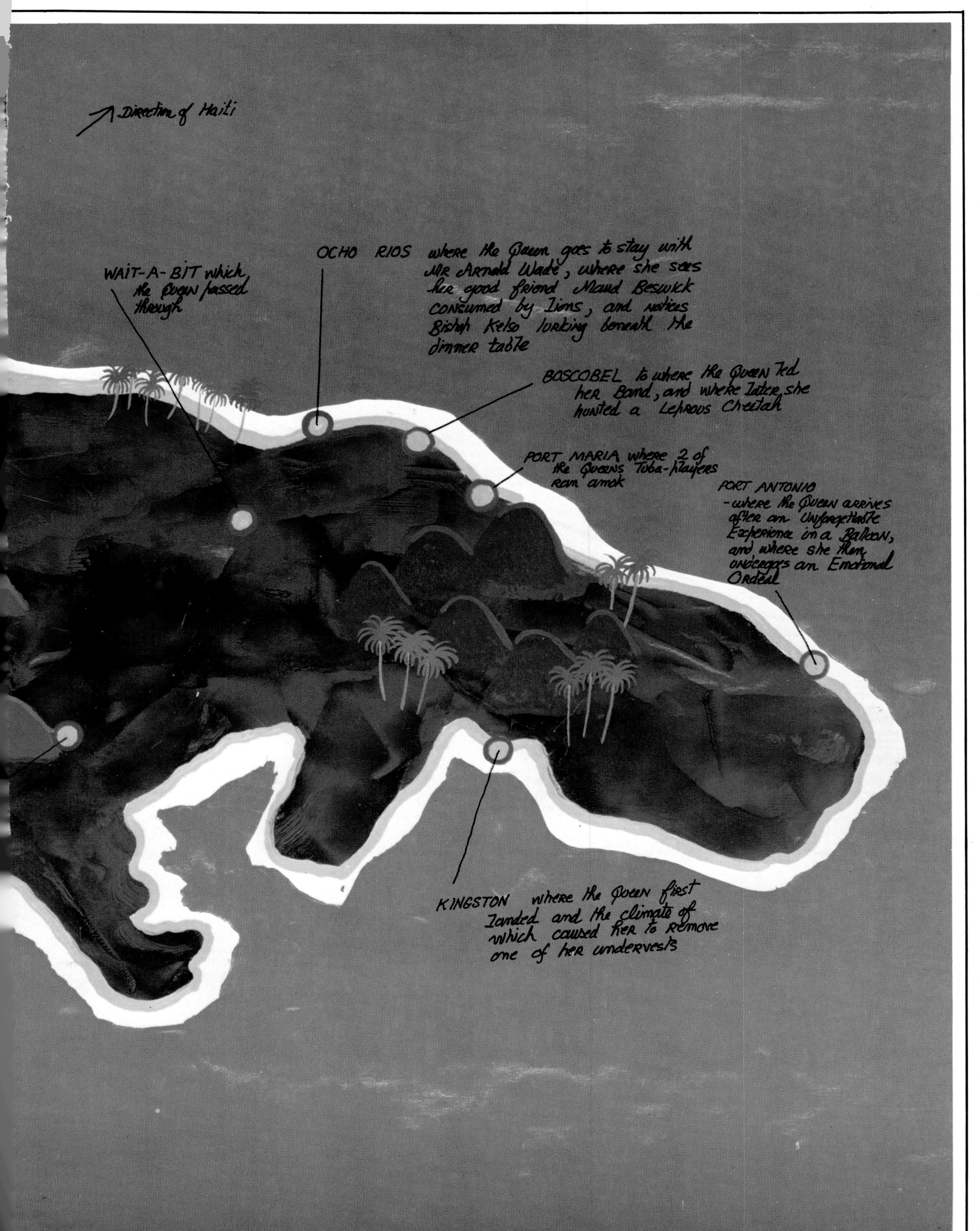

Direction of Haiti
WAIT-A-BIT which the Queen passed through
OCHO RIOS where the Queen goes to stay with Mr Arnold Wade, where she sees her good friend Maud Beswick consumed by Lions, and notices Bishop Kelso lurking beneath the dinner table
BOSCOBEL to where the Queen led her Band, and where later she hunted a Leprous Cheetah
PORT MARIA where 2 of the Queens Tuba-Players ran amok
PORT ANTONIO - where the Queen arrives after an Unforgettable Experience in a Balloon, and where she then undergoes an Emotional Ordeal
KINGSTON where the Queen first landed and the climate of which caused her to remove one of her undervests

In March 1972 I attended the party at the house near Montego Bay of Mrs Oscar Hammerstein II where new Queen Victoria paintings of mine were being shown in aid of Operation Friendship and the Hanover Charities. And there my very great surprise was to find myself being introduced to a very spry eighty-year-old Lord Braborough. Alas, though, an imposter – produced just for my benefit by friends in Kingston who knew of my obsession with the subject.

Shortly afterwards I visited the Jamaica Institute in Kingston to look at microfilms of back copies of the *Daily Gleaner* for the months of April and May 1871. There was one item only which had any relevance to the Diary – on 3 April, five or six days before Mrs King arrived in Kingston, it noted that 'Mr Arnold Wade, the American circus proprietor, has taken up residence at White River House, Ocho Rios'. So, the existence of one more character mentioned in the Diary was confirmed. But still I had nothing to connect Mrs King with Queen Victoria.

I then visited the Jamaica Archives in Spanish Town where repose all Volumes of the Annual Jamaica Legislature – that almost hourly account of government business kept by the Recording Secretaries of all the past Governors of the island. It, surely, I felt, must make some mention of – at the least – the instructions concerning the Queen's safety sent by Mr Gladstone to Sir John Peter Grant. It did not: for the simple reason that the 18½ missing pages in the 1871 (Part 1) Volume exactly coincided with the period of the Queen's visit to Jamaica. One could see they were missing – none too cleanly torn out – as all pages were numbered. And pages 167 to 185½ just did not exist. The entries for 12 April were followed immediately by the entries for 27 May. And even though a member of the Archives staff assured me that very few of the nineteenth-century Volumes were in anything like their complete or original condition (following the seizure and ransacking of the Archives building by the Dirty Beatty Mob in 1908) it struck me – concerning the omissions in the 1871 Volume – as being just too much of a useful coincidence. Those pages had been deliberately removed to prevent anyone from learning of the Queen's presence on the island.

Next, I decided to try Rattehall where Mrs King had stayed so long. And here I had more luck. Kenneth Diacre – Major Count Kenneth Diacre de Liancourt to give him benefit of his full name – had returned to the Rat Hall Estate (as it is now called) ten years previously, after a distinguished career in the Life Guards, to set about reviving the Estate's fortunes as a sugar plantation. He knew little of his great-grandfather – the Count Diacre with whom Mrs King must have stayed – except that he had had to leave the island suddenly and mysteriously in the early 1880s – some scandal that involved several of the leading families of the island. He promised he would write to his family in France and ask if, amongst the relics of his great-grandfather, there was any trace of the visit that Mrs King had made to his home. Though as Count Diacre, like Mr Arnold Wade, knew Mrs King only as Mrs King and not as the Queen I wasn't quite sure how this would help at all.

Six months later, after the Jamaican Prime Minister Michael Manley appeared to open the new Inter-Continental Hotel at Ocho Rios (and found nothing exceptional concerning my paintings of Queen Victoria in Jamaica which decorated the hotel's dining room), and just after there had been some publicity in the Jamaican and American papers concerning my quest for information about the Queen's visit to the island, I received a letter from an Enid Braborough of Miami offering me what she said was a complete copy of the Diary of Queen Victoria in Jamaica. For $10,000 she said it could be mine. I should send her cash and make no attempt to trace her. I wondered if this could be further alleged friends from Kingston or anywhere else for that matter trying to put another one over me. As I didn't have $10,000 to part with that easily I did nothing about it. Two weeks later I had another letter from Enid Braborough, this time from an address in Key West and enclosed with it several thousand typewritten words which she said were an exact copy of the Diary in her possession. She repeated her request for cash and that I should make no attempt to trace her. I had to know the truth, however.

And it was at this junction that I decided to enlist the help of my friend, the distinguished Victoriana scholar and commentator on world affairs, Richard Lubbock of Toronto. I asked him or his emissaries to find out what they could about Enid Braborough and, if satisfied by their discoveries, to purchase the copy of the Diary from her. Richard Lubbock himself went to Key West and spoke with Enid Braborough. Satisfied by her bona fides he bought the copy of the Diary from her – for a sum considerably less than she had originally requested – and gave me this brief report on his findings:

'Queen Victoria on her return from Jamaica gave her Journal to the person she trusted most in the world, John Brown, to read and look after. Unintentionally or otherwise she never retrieved it from Brown. On Brown's death in 1883 the Journal passed into the hands of his niece Patsy. Patsy (Mrs Palmetter) died in 1914 and bequeathed it to her son Hamish who *lived at Braborough* in Northumberland, and Hamish, when he died in 1954, left it to his daughter Enid Victoria, who had married a marine

biologist called Brady who worked for the University of Florida Marine Biology School on the Florida Keys and who died in an underwater accident in 1974.

'It would also seem likely that the original of the Diary was sold to or otherwise acquired by the Royal Family, possibly with Ld Goodman acting on their behalf, at some point between 1954 and 1974; and the copies which Enid retained were simply to enable her to raise some small sums of money in the event of any emergency (like, presumably, her husband's death).'

This was all very well, but I felt that while representatives of the Royal Family still denied the existence of any such Diary, Enid Braborough's confession was still not enough to substantiate Queen Victoria's existence in Jamaica. I really felt, most of all on account of those missing 18½ pages in the Jamaican Legislature, that I was up the traditional gum-tree.

* * *

Eighteen months ago I promised I would never do this. But this essays to be a serious work of scholarship, and there have to be times when scholarship and truth take precedence over promises. I made my promise to a very distant kinsman, whose great-grandfather was Ludwig IV, Grand Duke of Hesse and by Rhine. He married in 1862, Alice, the third child of Queen Victoria and Prince Albert. They lived in the Grand Ducal Palace at Darmstadt. One day, eighteen months ago, I was there with Herr Kreps, the Palace Archivist. I was telling Herr Kreps about my quest for proof of Queen Victoria's visit to Jamaica, as usual boring anyone who would listen. Herr Kreps, with a mysterious smile on his face, left the Library and returned two minutes later with a bulky black cardboard box from which he extracted one fine cream-coloured sheet of paper. It was, he told me, a letter from Princess Alice to her husband the Grand-Duke Ludwig. I started to read it: '. . . *Mama is still in Jamaica as "Frau König" and she writes that she has slept in the house of an American! ! ! – & has a Black Maidservant! ! !'* – those are the words I remember completely. I didn't have to remember more, though. Those few words were the proof I had been seeking these last seven years. My kinsman came into the Library at that point, saw what I was examining, took it out of my hands and chided Herr Kreps for having shown it to me; and then he extracted from me the promise I mentioned earlier.

Forgive me, dear and distant cousin. The proof only makes greater a lady who was already the greatest that ever existed.

J.R.

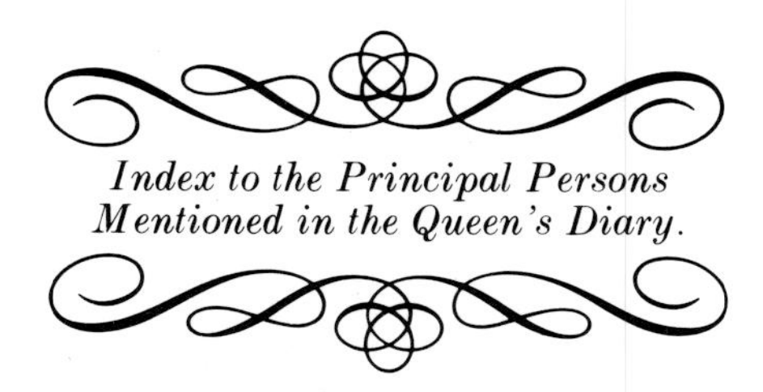
Index to the Principal Persons
Mentioned in the Queen's Diary.